MY MIX IN
SHORT STORIES
AND
POEMS

SHORT STORIES, POEMS AND MORE.

ANNETTE BAKER STOVALL

authorHOUSE®

AuthorHouse™
1663 Liberty Drive
Bloomington, IN 47403
www.authorhouse.com
Phone: 1 (800) 839-8640

This is a work of fiction. All of the characters, names, incidents, organizations, and dialogue in
this novel are either the products of the author's imagination or are used fictitiously.

Published by AuthorHouse 10/31/2019

ISBN: 978-1-7283-2389-3 (sc)
ISBN: 978-1-7283-2388-6 (e)

Library of Congress Control Number: 2019912256

Print information available on the last page.

Any people depicted in stock imagery provided by Getty Images are models,
and such images are being used for illustrative purposes only.
Certain stock imagery © Getty Images.

This book is printed on acid-free paper.

Because of the dynamic nature of the Internet, any web addresses or links contained in this book may have changed
since publication and may no longer be valid. The views expressed in this work are solely those of the author and do
not necessarily reflect the views of the publisher, and the publisher hereby disclaims any responsibility for them.

CONTENTS

Under Summer Skies

Under summer skies there is a pattern
that comes again with summer does matter.
Here do blue violets keep for bloom
at now green meadows keep is for tune.
Brown sparrows tan strut do struts well
as go hummingbirds of hum tunes to assortment dwells.
And right assortment we look between
sprightly sorts do how assortment seen.
When bush and boughs the sway when songbirds jig,
when local pansies due for chirps in the jig.
And should the rain will tap, tap, tap
it upgrades rain alike to keyboards rap, tap.
When we in touch with summer it makes clear,
this is that dainty as fair time of year.

ANALOGY

As now I look beside the spring youth,
Applause I'm here for starts on blend.
Ah, you have worth alike young
The mead of trick vaults to send

As if ere the moss expired
These delicate of blends must fast leap.
But trick vaults will mirror coarse gains
Shall soon with fringe and flap weep.

Last, I see no jolt how trick
Reflected in your value mound.
Ah, you match the spirits bloom
When birds are thick and sounding.

THE WOODS BEHIND US

We wondered if the woods behind us
would bloat like woodsy monster, near, living beside
where dwelled who undisputedly mate, kids and I.
Where times I looked against a window sill I'd spy
the spotted pelt hare scurry trace at handiwork back yard
containing carrot tops fresh row aligned with crop goods part.
His glad recess off hop where thorn limbs, he cared where search.
The garden snake thereabout seemed he slithered less he'd care
where he meandered mass in back woods or go anywhere just so his
for everywhere to roam take.
We could nights know the loud clicks were of crickets make
horn antennas play to mass for cricket toning heard.
Some creepy little wiggly things where tones occurred
we cared less of know more about that we should.
Wild brush made the mixed in grass won't generously grow in woods
fit for wild branches dangled bush and tree limb some fell free.
For truth, few average neighbor go there.
Except to go behind for make a plot unfettered with stiff weeds
and waste if one to plant a garden there.

No Haste For National Park

Manie upon sit down in favorite soft seat -- I just got back from doctor Tilman's office. He said he could not say why I have sharp stinging chest pains come and go nor why I feel so listless half the time. I get results from tests he ran in a couple of weeks. Why are you dressed in striped leggings and colorful stripe cap? "Why ask me why. We agreed on going today to Joshua Tree Park."

Yes, now I do remember. We planned it for today. That was a week ago. Today, I don't know, his reply.

"No matter. I changed my mind anyway. I read in the paper after you left for doctor office this morning, that Joshua Tree Park along with some other National Parks across California, are shut down because of safety concerns over human waste. People have trashed, vandalized, and damaged park along with park vegetation. Some have even left champagne bottles strewn about. One hiker broke his leg on the glass. All that with strong waste piling stink on bathroom floors and roads near, no solution but shut down several parks, especially the campgrounds. Why do they not staff workers and guards on site all day long everyday?" I can't answer that. I say too many people visit National Parks to do any good. Should only a certain amount allowed on those campsites. "Well, maybe. I say guards and more workers best. Anyway since that park out of the question, I've decided we picnic in canyon close. You not ailing this minute, can't hurt for man of 39 out somewhere, clear summer day like today."

I'm not convinced but okay.

Afternoon with canyon—"This is where we chose, right Manie?" You chose this one. I preferred canyon farther down off the highway. "We both chose. Nevermind. Sit here this table good. I so remember playing here when a child. My parents brought my two small brothers and me here times for campout and hike. I was 8 then. My now 34 years still remember. Were only a few picnic tables for family meal, 2 the most." Still few. Four not many. Stella, do you recall that outing we were on when a splattering of seemed like 50 bees flew over our heads loudly buzzing and frightening our group of five people? If not for that bug insecticide on our arms we could have got stung. "Yes, I do remember. That was that campsite grounds they dutifully comb and no stray bottles around grounds to our agreement." What is this pie you baked? "My easy bake zucchini pie. It makes the crust as it bakes. Thought I'd try it out on you. Baked it early this morning." Good taste. I like it, also your deviled eggs. "Glad you like both. Even I can't say which tastes better."

On their hike--"You don't have the ache now do you?" No, none this very moment. "Good. There used to be wild parsley growing where grassy area." What grass area? You see grass, I see thick brush, stones and rocks. "We passed it few yards back at baseline we crossed. Keep your eyes open. Before rudely interrupted, I had started on saying wild parsley growing then. Wild flower upshoots climbing, too. Now area mainly interspersed with patches of bent grass turning frayed by sun or droughts occur. Some blade stems look more like splinters for burn. Mama used to pick the wild parsley back then more greenery seen. She loved cooking with spice and herbs. What a good cook. For that, quick tempered, though not overmuch, poppa even gave her credit."

"Look, a blue jay."

How can you tell. Stella, it's too high up to even see. "I can tell. I know a blue jay when I see one."

"There's the cave I remember plundering through with some kids. All we took were colored rock trappings. We can look, too, plunder a while."

After minutes inside cave - - "What was that noise I heard? Sounds like bear or lion yawn."

Bears nor lions like to be around where people. I heard something, too. Probably a noisy rodent I think we heard.

"Too loud, I say, for just a rodent. Manie, you contradicting me again. Time we head back. I'm getting scared."

CALIFORNIA BLUES

I look upon spring my quest
"Why won't it rain?"
No lighting quick flash or storm
"Why won't it rain?"

There's a track of white clouds,
"Why won't they burst?"
West perimeter drought this year
Is cruelty at its worst.

Oh, it does, will rain
For not enough time.
And radiant sun casting silly grins
on pavement dirt and grime.

Few the blond spills rap the bird bath
heaps far low water.
When will amber fields and farm lands
heap stack as they ought.

As global warming takes its toll,
Some plants wet as dry.
The farms parched with little rain,
Farmers complain and cry.

When the drought would suddenly end,
people do not know.
Unless rain falls with long rush
again, some grains will not grow.

Oh, the animals would drink
but desolate streams are dry.
They would eat the fodder of mead more
but large tuft of grass is shy.

Oh rain where close are you?
Creation predicts for due
your approach. All West Coast so
awaits your wet timbre due.

GRATITUDE

It was a Friday morning
after breakfast. Of course I had had
my physical food but my brain
still hungry debated for more.
Looking for brain provision works
I matched self to chemist in his lab
looks for the perfect mix
to work for gray mouse runs.
Suddenly I spied inside front room
the little square pamphlet stood out
in line with the square coffee table top
put like the wood grain desk.

Right then the front page screamed
the loud stated add pitch,
*Slash Cholesterol with Cinnamon.
Thankful enough, I soon push for more
inside the little booklet pages.
*Walk off belly fat fast
*12 steps to keep mind and body young
*End headaches now
*12 new Superfoods for women
*Sleep better tonight
were some heavyweight titles list between pages add rambled on;
*Live longer with Pizza and
*Lift your spirits with Chocolate bar
sounded thankfully good. So too could
*If your memory recall skips,
many a case ranks for normal.
Brown sockets wide as mothballs,
my eyes next flashed on high blood pressure.
One man reduces his with celery though.

But would that do for me?
My next impression appears to be
grateful for brain food served.
Would just read for the most part work?
Suddenly it screamed, Buy the whole book!

People Go Here

"Water, soda, bomb pop anyone?"

"I'll take a bottle of water." Abigail paid the sales vendor and heads across the promenade walk.

"Hi Floyd, How is business?"

Not so good, his dark African lips replied. I have been trying to sell my creative art piece for months, almost a year. I could use a haircut. Some days I leave before 5 p.m. instead of sit here all day.

"Me too. Some days I leave around 2p.m. It gets hard, too, trying to sell paintings out here."

I used to sell paintings, too, that almost nobody bought. So I decided on create something nobody else here selling.

"I give it that. It is unusual, nothing I ever seen out here or anywhere far as that goes."

A stranger came near where Abigail standing beside the makeshift outdoor counter the object sitting on.

"I never seen one like it either. It looks like an avantgarde style set in concrete. I can see appears to be a face, an arched gateway, a radial tire. What did you make it from?"

I made it from diverse items I found outside here and there. People see what they want to see. One lady saw a water fountain squirting water pitched high like it reaching high into heaven as if to remove itself from what's defiling humans and elements here on earth.

"I did not see all that he surprisingly said. I suppose one can see just about anything. How much you asking for it?"

Three hundred.

"That is a lot you ask. But I think it is worth it. I have a wide mantelpiece I can sit something like this around 3 ft. by 2 ft. You did a good job of cementing the parts just so, even the sand and seashore look right. I could come back tomorrow bring the $300. Nothing much I know of California since new here. But if I say I will come back, trust me."

They always do say that Floyd said suspiciously once the stranger left. Do I cheer or cry?

"I would be happy or hoping patiently. People sell me the same spirit boosting story. Sometimes they come back, other times disregard return. See what of tomorrow. I think he will return. He sounded sincere, in earnest."

She went on her way to a long restroom line, pulling her wheels tote bag filled with paintings and greeting cards she had painted.

Suddenly the aged woman her hair gray and partly black who stood in front of her said, "Don't stand too close to me. I got robbed that way once." She looked African but could have been Mexican.

"I'm sorry. I never do stand too close unless the line like it is now. I'll try to step back a little. How did you get robbed?"

''Some 2 fellows. One stood beside me getting my attention with talking while the other one in line behind me picked my summer pants pocket, lifted my wallet I never missed till hours later I got cash for something. And what with watching all the wares I brought for sell, I never checked my pocket." Abigail could see she then too had items in the wheel cart packed full she looked down at every few minutes.

"That is awful it happened to who seems a nice lady," Abigail said sadly.

"Yes it was too awful. I could say the same about you being nice. Some people get angry when I tell them don't stand too close. Not you. You took it right."

That was Abigail's due to folk who knew her as the brown skin African American, her seasoned middle age not likely to deliberately be unkind to anyone.

She went from restroom area thinking she would have to keep an eye on her cart wheel tote she kept her wallet inside. Passing by sea waves jumping water on hot sand white sail boats in the distance, she settled for mid-way empty spot for display her paintings beside promenade walk. Being fearful folk may buy a painting from another artist, she figured some would first walk the promenade at least half way. "Hello" she said to the group walking by while she spread cards on the pad she had immediately placed over sand before she propped her paintings against whatever stood them up. Her cards as well as paintings were of her own making. Some people said hello while others turned heads and kept walking. Soon a homeless young man sat on the sand next of her where each space numbered on the concrete walk. He set out something she leaned over her chair to see.

"Are those magnifying glasses?" she said curious to know.

He said, yes, and she bought one. She reasoned she could use it with adding little touches to her paintings. She thought about how homeless people come here too for sell whatever the item even if just weird writings on scarred paper. This was the one beach the hybrid medly of people mostly Mexicans, blacks, and few whites came to sell something. Some sold much, others less. People who brought in clothes from somewhere, it seemed to Abigail they sold much. Creative art persons like her could not sell much. If she asked why, folk say out of money. Some say they don't buy art from just anybody. And she had earned A's in art at college. There should have been the store somewhere artists could sell their skillfully worked art.

Next day she spoke with Floyd, his dark frame face she guessed at age 35 now clean shaven and cropped hair cut looked orderly.

"I see someone got paid."

Yes, the man bought my rare art innovation this morning. Afterwards, I went to the nearby barbershop.

"I told you he seemed sincere. I hate to say I told you so."

Yes, you did. For that I feel I owe you a share of the sale money. I won't say right now. I first have bills to pay. We'll see by weekend. Will you sit here with me today, some other days too. I feel you brought me good luck.

"I'm sorry I can't. I have a special place I love to sit. Do good with your well earned money. Save some for the weekend."

She waved bye and walked to her space for unload the paintings. There she sat with umbrella in hand for break the heat beside surface abutted promenade people walked.

"Water, soda, cookies, balloon anyone."

THE BETTER YEARS

In the summer of our life,
then were the better years.
Then evenings we alone we loved more
when life was good with youth years.

We laughed where we held hands
beside the stalks in grass yards loom
for we knew most we were beloved.
Adored when summer song birds croon.

Everything we did was fun.
Even in summer and soon autumn rife.
We pondered not of what ageing steals.
For these were the better years of life.

Sweet Mary

Sweet Mary is her jolly gal
jolly and one fair of face.
So hard to say of others look stoic pal.
Just ask her why so.
"I have this even some leprechauns long.
I charm of charm I love it gentles effective my charm.
You narrow hear of me for crude pixie tongue.
I laugh Oh so genuine real chimes my laugh
alike to no dryad of mythical islands do."
With glee advancing glow like made for young eyes aglow
even like the night is dim yet still admits hue,
you ask me why, how though.
She is the Mary her Merry merry,
She frolics her sugar and spice.
She is glad Mary Merry
loves convey joy to life!

This Fat is a Dilemma

Maxine upon coming inside: I just came from the gym. Someone fell off the treadmill and had to be rushed to the hospital. She hit her head so roughly on so rigid you know how stiff that gym floor.

Benita: Did she hurt anything else?

Maxine sitting down: I don't know. It happened so fast, and then they rushed her to the hospital. Last minute in the rush I could see who she was.

Benita: Did you ever meet her, introduce yourself?

Maxine: Yes we met said hello. She was a rather shy, timid young lady did not have much to say. I envied her tall and less bulging figure. I don't know why she bothers working out inside a gym. Right now, I wouldn't like to be her placed on that hospital guerney.

Benita: Neither would I. I don't see why you envied her though. I tell you all the time, you look great how you look now.

Maxine: Thanks for the compliment. You know me. I'm not easy to please. Too much fat if I pinch or even see on my waistline indicates to me I must do something. Walk, exercise with weights or at the gym. Other times I just diet. I've tried multiple diets. At times they work, other times they don't.

Benita: I, too, have gone that route. I wager everybody at one time or another is troubled with weight gain and how lose the fat arms, big gallon gut whatever, unless they are the slender fashioned Barbie doll no mentality prone to worry.

Maxine: Amen to that. Fat is a hell of a problem. And what's more, if you do lose weight, damn fat comes right back again.

Jenny from across the room: Look at me. At 160 pounds, I'm fat for a 17 year old teenager. I don't let it bother me. Just let it flap where it hangs.

Maxine: I would not brag about it much. Have you seen those fat people on one tv show. They weigh 600lbs. or more.

Jenny: Now that is fat. I don't figure on having any forward inclination of becoming that fat.

Maxine: I feel sorry for people like that and know something about how it feels to try losing weight without success. I even reached the point no matter how I lift weights, walk long blocks or diet, I won't lose the stick to hip stuff.

But damn, did you see the case woman over a thousand lbs, lost her life right there on tv. One day she was alive the next day dead. The doctor should have had her lose a lot of pounds before he operated to shorten her stomach. I've seen doctors do that on another show. Hopefully, what happened to her won't happen again.

Benita, call me later after your dinner over. I'm heading home to eat my soup and salad.

Is There Good News?

Is there any good news?
Hurricane Nemesis tore down.
Glad I slept through it
in another town.
Ferocious fire tore through homes
of my coastal state range.
I know how damning smoke flame.
The cost of gas goes up.
Complication if that's not enough
rape and real aches, war still.
Cheers to whose guide does no harm.
Too many homeless fear the storm
malady common with live outside.
Be locally aware sad fame
Green House gases go yet untamed.
Too, wife and child abuse.
I bought the air fryer
but can't eat much food, life's bane.
Too many black men no weapon
to shoot still shot down slain.
Is there any good news.

KEEPING GLORY

Do not let doom on parade dismantle glory
from every chapter writing on your story.
That shady march will help and sometimes will not
defines revolving case people living no doubt.
Here is where you cheer or have much less to shout.

The chapter that parades in your life today
could be changing epic brightness to mirror clay.
Still, always looking for the better summary
could lighten up blue episode some may run from.
You bless the next theme foretells right outcome.

Do not let doom on parade dismantle glory
from every chapter writing on your story.
Some choice theme more adept at beaming the light.
Most you will find it limits the entitlement.
But do not let the real glory soon out of sight.

PRESCRIPTION GRANTED

She said to me one sunny spotlight day,
"Why do you read and write poems?
I can not understand much of what poets
they write, myself." Why indeed.
Once the young British doctor for one
gave up practice medicine for just avowedly practice
only his poetry. He said, "My toil expressly
is for man's joy." Now that is a doctor hooked
far as I never heard of one hooked on poet medicine for human minds.
Today even some psychiatrists prescribe too
for addicts instead of stay hooked main
on drugs, they get hooked essentially on poems
like "The Road Not Taken" by Robert Frost
or on some other soothing verse.
The metaphor or two won't hurt
and could nail dim in sadness over size like
a red barrel you piercing blue gaze fast
than fingers open a white envelope.
Metaphor or not, poetry lives for designing read
those flip the pages near to silent gusto burns
A fine tune plays it over unto it stays
revolving why rhymers write poems.

She Lived 15,638 Hours In A Car

Here she was a senior soon evicted from her apartment after her husband lately died. Now she lived in her son's garage. Not long afterwards upon moving, he could not bring her along with the family, so he gave her his old make car for temporary residence. *The almost 2 years she abided* living in his car, she lived through weather was hot, rainy, sleet etc. and as a consequence contracted pneumonia. She slept with feet crammed against a car seat which only led to walking with a cane. Still expecting some solution, she wondered why she had to go through this ordeal. And if forever she'd stay in some strange backlot still inside the car jam packed with clothing she brought along. She had no friends willing to take her in. And had to use her meek S.S.A. check each month to pay for furniture storage and pet kennel rent, so much so, that she had almost no money to last the month for food and high gas rate. No wonder she looked sad! Later, it was about time the long awaited law allowed people without residence (and only these) to attain a section 8 voucher. Here was her chance. She turned her life around with take the first apartment allowed her and her pets residence.

Here, she is being foresighted when she wishes many a baby boomer a better future would be enough to get some things done that a generation ago foregone you could not accomplish. Good Luck! You'll need it.

A Voice from the Past

I was the one who worked and helped
them fix each copper plate.
My dreaming firm palm to stretched the iron frame,
not far from truth every rung it touched
inscribed some truth should always be
hands linked where grouped these nation states
gripped strong for liberty.

The year was '86 and did for Bartholdi
his matron grand, proud lady for the switch
from port to harbor bay.
Black hands, I'm dreaming, to help lifted top frame,
I thought of here group, if rank and help if race
they'd all be free.

Long age by the base for our national scope,
stubborn, this love as for race won't cease;
Since race to cope designs for overload brief,
And race to score do fight and weep.
And if by God one race will all be free,
then, long live Liberty.

Living on the Edge

She had it all ready. Table cloth spread over hard wood table, meal put just right in the center for pleasant evening for them to dine. She knew to have things in place, knew him for prone to inspect something even if covers on beds in bedrooms.

What would he say. He arrived home around this time 6 o'clock evening for dinner. Upon hearing the front door shut, instinctively she turned to lay eyes on the well built frame fast standing where still in the kitchen she placed table utensils. Hi dear, how did your day go?

"Same as always. Not much goes on with metal repair except

work. What is that meal I see. Smells dreadful. What made you even think to cook that? Haven't I told you I don't no way like asparagus no way it cooked. You deaf and all out brain dumb too? Now clean up this mess. All you good for anyhow."

Alright. Just don't slam all our dinnerware on the floor. To her nothing smelling dreadful.

He had a knack for be insensitive unkind. She was glad their two children in back room with video game action could not hear din of dishes crashing. Awkward times they heard him raise hell, they so numbed with fear.

She could recall him different years ago before they married and several months afterward. He bought her gifts and on occasion, flattered her with compliment or two. How had he become harsh so. Man her husband so vexed her till live around him like living on the slanted cliff edge she never understood how slip she made ignited his gripe flared up. She could hear, in the background his yell, "Serve me salad, pasta, anything with the meat. Never that awful tasting other vegetable. If I do correct you of that again, you won't like it."

She knew that meant something unwanted. And knew also she was how timid, underserving of the abuse he scarred her with. His bruising left black and blue marks along with darkened eyes known for battered wife syndrome, term she rather not be a part. What could she do but ditch this hell again. Flee her blue collar man's luxury home built on outskirts fine suburbs. True, she had left before taking the kids. Over the ten years they dwelled, theirs had been the love ran hot and cold like flows from water faucet into galvanized tub. She should first go stayed gone.

Why had she come back. "Don't go back," her parents warned fearing the worse.

She swears to leaving him, go where genuine the love between the small brick home her parents live. Reality with them will show they care too much to frighten off who fed on abuse. She vows in leave once and for all for good. Will her vow stand?

WHEN IRIS THE MAMMOTH CUE

When iris the slate it cued,
A purple lack went with me pursuit
If even at close by the block
Where upright stood the shade of case
The gray mantel indented base
Where carving dents the marble art;
Or if benear one blue to be lake
A halt could latch of shoe and take
No anxious veer or step I'd gander
Where drab for duck and geese appeared.
And by the shade not just for bench,
If in that 'mount for bonny grass
There also how endearing mote
As if remained for dull mope.
I Wondered, then, if slate I'd feel
But would add up with no hope deal
And stall my wait for the ample turn
Would right the iris way sum.

Fade Moment Lost

If day in bright for clearly exhaust,
Then dunnish night in for the fault;
Creeping around in dull gray house,
Crawl in the maze like dust tail mouse...
The lavender of nights with just I know who;
The jasmine lights too far I can't pursue.

Till, yet, through lights I'm nudged a bit,
Vaguely overt and deep gloom counterfeit.
Frail lucid light, the past of once tossed,
It was best kept dun memory lost.

Agreement Late In Coming

Jason is a cheerful dark skin man greets people with a smile. He keeps diligent about coming to work as an accountant in simple fashion suit. His white shirt is nothing but immaculate. Though Mark, his office peer is outspoken he also is fun to be with.

After a busy morning with work, they chat on way to lunch. "I moved out from parents last week. I'm living in a white neighborhood I hope it less for prejudice. Seems good so far. My apartment just what I wanted, the rooms not very much large or small and carpet everywhere."

Not in the kitchen, unless you want gooey grease for floor wax. "Oh come on. You know I meant almost everywhere. Best of all, no mother around to pamper me." They exit elevator to walk outside down steps.

"There is that gal I told you about. That is heaven on two feet."

Looks pretty good to me too.

"How can I come to know her, Mark. I never had sex, never even been on a date."

Thirty years old and never had a date. You must be kidding or you lived on a no women allowed planet.

His words rang true but absurd to Jason inside Mark's car.

"I was not saying I never been with a female. I have messed around as a teenager, but that was kid stuff, nothing deep."

All I can tell you Jason is to go introduce yourself, ask her name. If she gives you her name and telephone number besides, you scored first base. If not, you scored for in the dugout, waiting for what next. Maybe you can reach first base, at least.

They exit Mark's car. Inside the restaurant they order lunch. Why so long living with parents before moving?

"I wish I knew. Maybe because mother pampered me so. Afterall, I was their only child. That much she never lets me forget. She bought pajamas for a gift once. "Just for my only son." I said Mama, what do I need with more pajamas. I have 10 pairs already?"

Ten, that's ridiculous. Don't worry, I can donate the others to charity.

"That would leave me with just one pair." But it's the best pair, made with spandex. Who knows, I may buy more. Say another 5 pairs. "That's mama for you. She came to my apartment just last week, looking for dust on wood tables that she could wipe away. Then took smudged shirts nearby to laundromat. Mama would spoon feed me if I let her. At dinner when living with dad and mama, she came up with one day, "Taste this" and smiling courteously with guide the spoon to my lips. I said no to braised carrots and smiling back just as courteous. One spoonful could lead to another."

How do you put up with a nosy wanna be spoon feeder?

"I don't always. My mother is my first love if I even estimate no dispute in she will visit often. She visited twice already in one week. Sometimes I entertain the idea of jokingly holler beside the door, "I'm not at home." She knows very well she is welcome, just use welcome with discernment."

"People think black mothers do not dote on their kids. I say they do, especially an only child like I am. Black mothers love their kids so much they give them funny nicknames like Pookie, Little Gramps, Sweet Pea. Mine let a Sweet Pea visit me once. I just could not say much. Everytime I tried to speak, my tongue sunk back in my throat, would not get up. I was 17 then. We love our mothers too."

They headed back to work after lunch and worked till closing time at 5p.m.

Jason said goodbye to Mark as they went separate ways. In the garage his car parked he saw her again. That heavenly appearance gal he wanted to meet in her hot pink mini skirt and standing by her cardoor posing there for open. Suddenly, he went close like Mark said he should go introduce himself as Jason and got a surprise when up close he discovered he knew this pretty dark skin gal from High School.

I'm Julie. I think I know you, too, from Wilburn High. You spoke to me a couple of times but had nothing to say. You flexed your arms a lot and walked with your chest stuck out as if you made for strength training.

"Me flex? The only flexing I do now is with long bending over account keyboard."

"On second thought, it was me. Better it been me flexing than some other boy now a man thinks he has Superman muscles."

Why is that?

"Because I'm dying for a date."

No time for die on me now. Who knows what comes with make 2nd base. She said yes to date as he gave a hip twister jig she thought looked funny.

As for him sitting in a dugout, it sure would not be him. They set a dinner and movie date for the next night.

Five Celebrated

We were 3 gone there
and half way gussied up.
The man in teal blue shirt
the wife in flared out light pink skirt
the 4 year old how garbed slightly bold.
For spur of the moment reigned
in their attend request.
We were there in accord with no tube hats,
no flash room into red and white streamers.
Abode told where the started on plan
by spur of the moment came.
Still 3 were propriety elated.
I knew to these glad parents their gift
their only one daughter of 2 years
was much delight much like the singular jewelry type
you only to receive once in life. To her we all 5 of us
we made loud noises blowing cheerfully into
the stiffer crafted plum red paper horns
between sing Happy Birthday.
A quiet 2 year old made random dents where
in savory her eye pleasing cake slice.
A few years later she died.

I Made A Difference!

The small band of runaways who hid and huddled themselves behind the trees in that long dark night, had uneasy thoughts I'm sure. Would they be caught only to be brought back home again? Would they escape their piteous plight? "Shish! Not a sound from anyone!" my voice warned. I knew how the ungraceful rude risks and struggles they faced on the trail could all turn into the punishment befalls them worse if they caught.

Soon the men who were out for catch our band were in short eyesight, gone. Still, we must be of eyes and ears in keen attendance as undispirited we traveled on with sometimes cr4wling, sometimes skulking through snags and rustic grime in crumpled woods. To people living in the area, their escape would be the undebatable sign their leader, Black Moses, had struck again.

Now, when I left home after being hit in the head by something my husband threw at me, I never thought I would become this iron willed leader of people who needed iron will and unswerving hands to guide them if even a black woman's. I had time to think, though. I found some Quakers who were willing to hide me in their attic until time to travel to the next stop-over. People, upon reaching my north destination, I was too happy to be there, I'm telling you! But I never forgot about others who were still suffering under stern task masters. After so long an age with black women cook, clean, be nurse maid and slave dishwasher for massa's house besides toil in the fields where under blazing sun a man's whip cracked gashes in dark men's back, after so long with suffering I could sense blacks were ready to step up the rung from just be underdog.

It was then I came back south to help some of them who were slaves unafraid to leave the plantation because they thought they might be caught. I helped them escape by way of the

Underground Railroad, a foot path with stop-overs on the route. The Quakers and others were good about hiding us in their attic where they fed us also. People, we were so cramped! and somehow we braved the stillness.

Now, never in my broadest imagination did I imagine a black man in the 21st century would become president. Gracious Goodness! That is real progress! and I'm pleased I was a ground-woods precursor to that progress. Now, over 300 slaves were freed from the south to reside in the north through this route. Proud of who I was, I was Harriet Tubman.

Note To Cousin Passed

When you were pronounced gone
I wondered of why the young man.
I surmised you passed by Jupiter illumined star
with all its moons,
Mars with all its crescent shape disks.
And just for be with everlasting accredits one
that entity men say on the throne.
You could not to Hades unaware have flown
You were too caring of me for that,
she said in her journal part.
I lose nothing deserving of import
my dear cousin.
How right you were for the visible star
had fallen from a distance to where deserving
here always
in the crevice of my heart.

OPPOSITES ATTRACT

She loves to wake to coffee brewing,
He loves to wake in time start it brewing.
She loves to dress just right chill or sun,
He loves go in the wind, head no hat on.
She loves quiet for autumn dark she dines out,
He loves stay in by fireplace burning stout.
She loves how lyric jamboree with eve's New Year,
He loves next day game scores on tv clears.
She loves his kinky jokes if even some not funny,
He loves crumb put in corny joke she thinks fun.
She likes her sweet treat, he likes his meat rare done.
They both look cartoonish couple in blue jeans torn.
Yet they mate swell for say "in love still."
Which all goes to show opposites attract will.

ESCAPE PENDING

They had been through it before, yet, here they were again disturbed by the inferno still in sight. They could see in the distance how the blaze went shooting the flames torched brush and mountaintop shrubs, devouring whatever green resemblance they had. The family kept vigilant by the window inside livingroom had lights on. They had no desire for sleeping unless the sleep brief. They peered through the glass often and could even smell the faint puffs of smoke wafting underneath the window sills.

Margeret asked her husband, "How long can we keep up the vigil? It's getting late?"

Regretfully, as long as we have to. This waiting and watching makes me almost scream, "God or somebody do something." Cause this freak disaster deed to disappear. It's been 3 days already. I wish this was a dream I could awake from. One thing if anything to be glad about is we live on a hill we can focus gaze across the highway for if the fire getting worse. Those flames riding up like leaping from under a giant cauldron.

"If they do get worse, Frank, fireman or somebody will alert us of the danger in time for evacuate. When we lived in Santa Duran, we were alerted in time to evacuate in a hurry. We had our suitcases all packed and in the car trunk. Too bad we had to leave the paintings on the wall. What 's worse is two neighbors down the way died. They waited till the last minute and got choked by the smoke while trying to leave through that murky haze building each smoke film. People should have known fire that huge covered the whole of woodland's north side not soon to burn out. A couple of our friends died then too. I miss them still."

Folks do die. I wish I could fathom which is worse. Dying of disease or death by fire or toxic murky smoke.

"Death by any means gets dismal, Frank, though I rather not be damned. Is this the holocaust we heard about. I don't relish that happening. Another more days could come to that. Look at it. Debacle inferno yet strong with blazing. Go down, burn out! blasted blaze still shooting day and night! Turn up the air conditioner! We should not be damned to die from scald air and fire too. We like living here."

Could l butt in?

"Of course, Junior."

Why did you move way out in this wilderness?

"Your father should answer. He most wanted live here."

Well, son, I just could not like city living, shops everywhere. People could stray into where decent looking neighborhoods we might live. Besides, land here was flush with trees, green grass, and flower growing bushes, unlike our Cypress trees lately turning dry. Your mother liked here too, after seeing everything.

All I can say dad is I like living not far out, I think. Since living through this make 2 woodlands ablaze, our living could be persuaded to go elsewhere, suburbia maybe.

"Is that a bear crossing the highway for this way? Quick, lock the garage. No bear is living here!"

I already locked it yesterday, dear. I doubt he will be all that bold to climb uphill this far.

I think I should go drive around, see if the fire abated any.

We heard nothing since 6p.m. news.

You right, we haven't heard. I know you a grown young man, but be careful.

After gone one hour Junior comes back.

The fire still blocks away and not yet under control. The fire

man would not let me see up close. He said nothing about escape. Looks like we could be stuck here for who knows how long.

FEISTY LADY

Her hair was like the pansies bloom
and will not brief the shuffle long.
And when she danced, her jig no wrong
with dance off heartbreak her gloom.

Her lips were hot as pepper-corn
and bright as red the pod spins heat.
Her fiery dish she did always eat.
Since June or chill the spin this warm.

Those were the days when youth so sweet
a feisty gal did sing and sway.
Though years have taken youth downhill they
yet left her pepper-corns to eat.

WHAT DID THEY DO

What did the boy do about who seated in front of him blocking his view? He simply took off her hat.

What did the man do about his new fashion hair-cut? He paid the lady barber anyway.

What does the government do with tax money? Spend it.

What did the wife do when her husband up and left'! Found her another playmate.

What did the cat say to the mouse? Dinner time--for me only.

Why did the inebriated sot order a hamburger at the police station? Because the police station had a side window like restaurants.

What did the homeless do to get where they stay without a bathroom? Beats me.

What did the snarling dog say to the cat? Get ready to make haste.

How did the little lad get inside the theatre? He walked in.

Where did the beach-comber go after dark? To sleep.

What did the woman shopper say to the would-be thief? I just spent everything.

How did the wrong crooked cop get caught? He was packing luggage looked like filled with money.
What case is the case of the blues? The case of times we fail. What did one woman do who lived with an abusive mate? She shot him.

What did the little girl with lemonade stand.do one spring day became hot? She left it standing till sun going down.

What did the vegetarian eat when hungry? Veggies, fruit, nuts, and substitute meat.

What did some people do who tried over and over without success? Tried again and blamed the system.

Why did the ventriloquist dummy say "Hell-no" everytime? Because that day he didn't care to say hello.

What did the burglar do who locked himself out? Jimmied the lock. Where did the hours go? In circles around the clock with the hour
hand.

Why did more than one law offend us? Because they took away more than one freedom to do.

Love Names

Ann loves one and one well much.
Mabel she loves three this much.
Bernie flirts with bar the love to Minnie due
if Juanita, one, a stand in close view.

SALLY

Gee, did you ever meet Sally,
house in the alley.
She's a sweet Sally
greets you with a smile.
She welcomes even timid guest
and makes redundant no request
into what's on your mind.
Be it odds or of serious duress
she's all ears.
Goodness, she can harvest high yields begin
between she angles ear to hear.
Her bliss with empathy attacking worst stress
when heard easily what gets her worked up.
Or else tears flooded chest.
Gee whiz for her delicate soft touch
she offers if stay long enough
a cup of coffee or tea
with fig or fruit other cookies
won't need for doughnut.

After He Reached The Summit Cliff

After he reached the summit cliff green,
He climbed the hill held none before.
Over the heap and treading rock for seen
And glad for, now, on best the hill floor,
He'd try get used to superb edges seen

Where this the green grasses as he'd will
Were fair and foremost as, here, their leaves.
But looks to side showed cares downhill.
And having space as for rest relieves
He'd hold with better slate fulfill.

And with right ledge he'd, even, now, been,
This he must stay while sad for slips.
Over the heap arid treading hard should gain
This he must keep where climbing with slips:
He must keep conscience ways remain.

Habit Wings of Distraction

Here was wailing fussy
    wings bare
Shifting loud vented strikes
    had verve.
His diving skittish quick
    and swift
Gyrating up plagued too
    my verve.
Soon I looked how next
    do survive
Hissing dived for chaff
    me tired
It so persisted
    from go.
Swatter set for swat it from room
    my resides
I thought to add it whack
    would place it null and deal
    me blot for noisy hiss again.
But missed more than twice
    who sly.
Thus I set him out fly
    from came
Where outlasting chaff
    gone by.
So be in life I flunked
    when I was tried
But great day when my ordeal
    I survive.

Signed With Love

Hello, Madge. Just saying I love you. Don't wait dinner. I'll be late. Love, Joe.

"Joe is so thoughtful. He left this note on the frig."

Does he always do this, Madge?

"No not always. He brings me flowers. chocolate candy and not just on birthdays. Sometimes gifts will come with a loving card. When he at other times leaves a note saying I love you in another place like my purse or coat pocket, it surprises me and cheers me up at the same time, just as he suspected"

What a husband you have. I wish mine that way. He never leaves me a love note. And only time he brings me a gift is after I remind him, you know, if birthday or anniversary on the way.

"Joe did not just become amiable after we married. He would sometimes address me with compliment or gift even before then. Once he gifted me a dozen doughnuts. I said Joe what will I do with a dozen. I can't eat them all at once. And if I leave them sitting on the counter too long, they could become dry and stale. Besides, it's not just 12 it's 13 an unlucky number."

Bakery salesmen don't believe so, he said. They sometimes add extra one to put a smile on your face and afterwards hope you come back for more. I could stay an hour longer, help you eat almost all. You never told me Madge he was that amiable. I did see you with a gift once after you returned from date with him. You showed me the card he wrote in and signed "With love, Joe." From all

I've seen, he is a nice fellow.

"Yes he is. If he was not who he is gentle, amicable sort, I would never have married him.

We've lived as neighbors a long time. You know how I am. I can't put up with too much stress. I expect the same of him even at my now middle age."

Not many men like that, believe me. How long have you 2 been wed? I forgot.

"Twenty five years. We married young."

Twenty five and he still composing romantic love notes and giving you gifts. That's almost unbelievable. And you have 2 children.

"Sounds bazaar, but it is the truth."

Well more benign days to you. Say did you read a while back about one older gent who was going to be locked up because of his wifes condition?

"No I don't believe so."

It happens after his wife of umpteen years died of a seizure ailment, the relatives inspecting her dead body, questioned her non-hygenic appearance blamed him for her matted hair, half clean shape and no care-giver. They brought complaints against him and promised to have him imprisoned. His lawyer soon dis covered the key to his freedom. His wife had left so many notes expressing her love for him all taped on room into room, that he never did see the inside of a prison.

"That is one impressive news bit, Karen. Who thinks of leaving love notes taped placidly smooth against house walls, and the old gent goes free."

Did you ever think of write a loving note to Joe "No, but after listening to that case so remarkable, I expect I soon will."

PLATONIC LOVE

Narcissus whose revering main he left
His pride whereon the yellowish flower
In that vain gaze awarding hour,
He marked the bloom for lonely self.
Himself, he all, adored to all gaze bereft
Of stem the pride off himself.

And Echo, his platonic love,
Had only been his sounding dove.
She marked the bloom forever to love him
Like an allegiance owns of who many
The battle, main, but dark victory
'When love of pride owns to none win.

I QUEST

As Susie Que, I'm close about rank
Shall know this question--
Before it gets 'round to crocus dank
Do void of much select
The while do mantles laid for who keen
Their tweet unto nebs yet stirred
Have it their now emphatic scene,
Why are the lips unheard?
And those so tiny we embraced
So early ways unheard
In other dusts have spring encased,
I bow to we should quest.
And search if due when babes next birthplace
Be to Him who drapes our due fall rest.

THEIR TEMPERED HOME

Here, fills the rooms with sound spirited
Belongs with saffron gray of mat warms floor
When voices blue and ill discreet all
Awarded sound within their threshold door.
And full groom rates the hall
When firework marshal they of blues overheard
The fire raised loud side the walls
This legal house for home;
Where if brim measure, full the spirit spark,
If long remains on burning edge coals
It gently needs the tepid bath warm
By the tepid brim long on short spark.

HAIKU

The fresh orange tree
Dangles of wealth we blessed with.
Tilt leans "Pluck my gold."

A mellow sunrise,
Fresh air, Peace, Prosperity...
Almost in evidence.

A field of popcorn,
The rippled maize amounts tall.
Will arms hold enough?

Never to drink fear,
Never to feed loneliness,
Fickle illusions.

A lasting friendship
It owns of disagreement.
Yet a flame aglow.

At last a rainstorm.
I'm glad for when it should pound
And glad for when it ends.

What the gloomy sort.
Dark shade loneliness the blues,
It sometimes long keep.

Autumn leaves fall fast.
Elder age years go quickly.
Never they return.

I was true busy,
Then sunlight blinked up and down.
All meant rest a spell.

A far distant love,
It hides from my view, but why?
Perhaps recall best.

This week I fell down,
Left my keys in front door twice...
What else could happen?

A day star withdrawn,
Performance deeds know endings.
I'm home free with dream.

Scattered autumn leaves,
They crack and crumble due times,
Like broke promises.

The rough go ladder,
Might lead guide up to success.
You start on one step.

Facing the hurdle,
Proof rings it over again,
Life is a challenge.

Serenity's flame
Bright, soothing, having warmth,
I come alive with freedom.

Spring sun is mellow,
When songbirds' blooms too outdoors.
Radiance how free.

Dewdrops this tender
Don't cling even to past wrongs,
Though minds remember.

In the candlelight
I see still your charm aglow,
A love reverie.

A perfect day scene,
Gentle sunlight with oak trees.
Young love is in bloom.

A down lady bug,
Hopes and red contents torn. Death,
A moan to regard.

Umbrella blessings,
Tilt me inside core to know,
For there rains enough.

An august new year,
A dream came true with fresh start.
Faith saw it coming.

Bright days, dim sunset.
Comes transformation in life
Altered emotion.

The blue nights, daydreams,
Her fantasies reign until...
Discovered her passion.

The route is dotted.
Now you see the stumbling blocks.
Try for victory.

Tracing with mankind,
Caring, sharing burden time
Alive for the conquest.

Did You Wake to Minstrel Piped

Did you wake to minstrel piped
had your venom smiling after plays
In ground floor dances when appraised the minutes
appraised for the bird chants come near Apollo?
And after charge in atmosphere remade a song,
refrain in child prodigy, his cup he stirred
to mimic, even, more tweets in surface realm
too marvelous margin wonders.
Then, noon perfumed how plays a minstrel right
who danced the nimble pipes to loud duets
retard of weak graces have in coast the wildest flute.
He strikes a fluted missive docks him near
where picks they sample, Hades revels in
short on brief wake cologne.
Though we must not lose of wake we held.
For we beheld minstrel how directed.
For since a song began
floor was held to who pipes
dance was held to verve
child was held to marvel
made poverty held defeat.

No Random Act

Lindsey--Hi Meg. Am I glad to see you. Have a seat. I heard about what happened.

Meg (sits down)--Glad to see you too. I spent a few nights at mother's house. I would have called but I was too upset after seeing what happened. I just could not get everything out of my head. And who to blame? Find the spare key better than some other way.

Lindsey (seated)--You had a spare key?

Meg--Yes, I kept it inside the little ceramic frog's mouth posing beside the short porch to front entrance. If Langston had been home that could have turned the tide, so to speak. As you know, instead I turned the tide on him. I just could not steady live with man the abrasive critic. He was. either Saying I was too fat, too non-committed to keep the house tidy or that I was too much a prodical. Naturally if you say I'm fat I'm going to spend a lot on make-up, clothes whatever makes me look body glamorous other than fat. And if the house untidy, grab a rag, work those rooms cleaning house beside me. But no, he left cleaning house all to me and reduced my spending allowance. For that I had to say Goodbye. Now I regret we separated.

Lindsey--You 2 never seen for argue much. And when seen you were just as boisterous loud and even more so at times.

Meg--I disagree to me that loud. As argument goes, he won over 75% of those. That much you never did see. What I was implying is if he had yet been living here at home, they may not have chosen our home. I had gone shopping, and what I returned to was furniture turned over, drawers pulled out, jewelry rifled through. All they took was a heirloom necklace with backside insig nia; had been handed down through decades. My mother wore it and her mother before her. I was comtemplating wearing it soon myself to family reunion planned. It's adorned with diamonds wrought in a somewhat huge oval face design. Why would anyone take that and that only? They broke the side door to get in. Someone really knew how to hurt a person. Why the necklace?

Lindsey--Gets beyond me too, Why.

Meg--And who was the perpetrater?

Lindsey--My neighbor said she saw a black man snooping around your door.

Meg--I don't see how she could tell since it was night when I left and night when I returned. Some people still exsisting for be racists. What do you think about me getting a dog for protection?

Lindsey--I'd think twice. There's a case of a man became infected with tape worms from either the dog licking his face or from him rubbing his cheeks against the dog's fur.

And a woman was petting her pet pit bull when he suddenly jumped up from her lap and bit off her lower lip. House training and vet bills also add complications. It's up to you. Besides, people keep letting their dogs, cats too breed too much when we already have too many.

Meg--I never heard so many negatives about dogs before. I'll think about what you said though. Could be good advice.

A few days later:
Policeman inside Meg's house--Ma'am we found who the perpetrator.
It was the man you were living with. We suspicioned it was him when we discovered your door glass broken from inside the house. Who else had a key! He just wanted to scare your his affection, back in his arms again. He admitted that much under interrogation. Here is the necklace. What he intended for it, doubtful even he knows.

SHE WAS RIGHT

She was right about him.
Mild and meek from day one
in line with gentleman tagged him
earmarked between gent and handsome.
Martha her friend, too, admired him.
His mean not disrespectful
at times mean is expected
in line with little regret.
Since here a man shuns disrespectful.
He brought her the string of pearl necklace
he had the fair presence of add lovelace
his words more of to the card.
She was right about him.
Not everyday unveiling such as him.
Could she ask for more
than love he showers her with is kind still
what she touched a kiss to twice at will.
She was right about him.
As right as Martha to face right side
to lie on when she be ill.

Let it Play

The aged man could sure cut a rug.
The sound was right and pitch ideal.
His quick out jig never mattered
each time gay steps his shorted out.
What's your pleasure?
Some say less loud,
some say up blast loud.
Some neglect to say.
What's your pleasure?
Could it be soothing love notes,
courageous, crude, bitter word refrains,
sweet revelry uplifting?
What's your pleasure to play?
It warms the heartstrings in some way.

SILLY WILLIE

It was how silly of Willie
with stores all around still he
to go downtown for pants.
And there do wacky his comedic dance
looked funny in the aisle
with tunes the store pleasure to play
Someone might say,
Oh, did that man dance really!
To some it was how silly.
But his was how humor the way
ran long with comical Willie.

The Story of Me

If you ask me where I came from, I came from the central zone. State of Missouri goes by nickname the Show Me State. Meaning tell me, show me what you have.

Lay the knowledge bare defines what I need. Or elsewise uttered this plainly, Show Me. Now hear to my show. I lived in the little bungalow house, Little rooms, little yard, grandparents paid the rent.

I had to live with no biologic parents being they braced separation well. I was good with little house I read books on front porch beside peach tree in the yard,

bed of daisies fresh rising.

Much was good though danged maletree did zip, provided peaches. Each daisy I picked with wish for stay fresh long. Wish for what you will, help reward come.

What's more, we moved from place to residence. Slept in attic, basement, shared the bed once. The room too small abated ease down to less ease. Last for one best mark to score, it scored for only one. We wedded, became 2 best for each other. And also moved from place to domicile. Then 1, then 2, then 3 for children born and moving with us to as if reborn from years passed a domicile reframed

a little bungalow rooms reforged, amazing me how the long yard poised the ripe lavender tree mulberries hovered over yard with leafy greens good feed I planted. The little vegetable garden we wanted even more in abundance, but neighborhoods more in abundance planted. We shared the bliss was ours and theirs.

But gloom in worse misery such you don't wish for, it happened.

Suddenly our one breadwinner gone like passed away died without say goodbye nor gave fair notice. And a young man besides. Oh how I was heartbroken!

And family bereft included this now 4 children. Regretfully, I never heard it announced, 'I do' again. No trailing skirt for the young mother. No future walk down the aisle. Was it because of mine presently a team of four? Would a mate accept me and my full package? They were a prime gift given me. What else did I have for me to show. Years have passed leaving me where now I'm with ' Eureka I've found it: another state alias.

Eureka, something excellent, something happiness, something good fortune.

Still I search each awakening for something found.

REFRESH THE MEMORY

Discerning is to know
Remembrance why it looks one way
Inspiring, mainly, of beam in focus
Against, again, the dull dank day?

Reserving corner seat for sun of sand
It browns me slight when dull dank waves
When, too, shell mussel of tans I understand
When pebbles under the forecast waives

Of cloud séance is now gone.
But I can look like, still, this full
Mainly, by my one thought alone
Mainly, by the one thought I mull.

Seduction I of bare for spring
Denudes my thought down to noon should care
What time I'll know the attitude swing
At arm about embraced me there.

"Hello There"

Those days when tints were boosting black,
Wide, it stood, wore short neck the stack
Allowed for mouthpiece essential near.
When rings changing to hum for buzz the ear
Who fierce to hold on as if to declare - -
"Hello, hello. Is anyone there?"

How quaint, color cast of purpose should now
The blossom pinks, the antique yellow
Hue cast on sounding all the fuss.
Applaud the fuss, loathe the so long buzz.
When piercings are for summon who cares,
We answer to the call of who calls where

The one outcome for chatter owns the talk
Saves mounds of notes and miles trek walk.
Now, tones the ring, quick visit for hear.
Unless dial tone trips hum to buzz the ear.
Whose urge to hold on as if then to declare
"Hello, hello. Is anyone there?"

LOVE

Love, Love, Love.
Is there marvel more sublime.
Love is good, Love is kind.
Mind for choosing Love kind over seed love blind.
Love in the mix should not void reap
Love is grand, fine unique.
Love wears the stuff goes the length.
Love rears the raised bar high
to now to reap what meant.
And how to tally a score,
Love rates high on result sets more.

I Remember It

I remember it still.
The tulips were glad rising where they stand.
We were happy with walking hand in hand.
I remember it still.
The wind was slightly blowing effortless blow
on cypress green tree.
When most we could see then just you and me.
I remember it still.
Passion in the air flamed enticement dance
when the music piped melody's beautiful romance.
I remember it still.
We sipped coffee in wee light cafe.
We eyed art gallery's vivid cast display. I remember it still.
It should not floor me could reminded may
you too remember it still.

THIS WALK TIME

"I'm so glad, Saddie, we started walking every morning like we do together. Cause when I go walking alone like I was, I usually somehow end up inside a restaurant eating breakfast sandwich or something."

"Same here. Food is such a savory tease! Anywhere you go there's a restaurant or store. You are so right. Even if you walk through the mall you find the same."

"And why so many restaurants. We can't always eat foods they serve, not much anyway. Eat healthy experts tell us. Eat right, drink right, take your meds and vitamins or take herbs, travel, exercise, climb the steep sidewalk hill."

"A hill? Cathy, it gets exacting just climbing steps."

"You know what I mean, do something. They even advise read a book half hour each day. Reading the newspaper is not enough. Of course, walking is always on the list."

"Sounds like me. I walked almost everywhere when I was young between age 11 and 18. To aunt's house, the movies, a long distance to school and back or just for the leisure of walking. Before age 14, I even walked to elementary school."

"Watch out for that crack, Saddie, could make you fall."

"Once I became adult, most walk habits succumbed to riding inside a car, at least until I began living alone. Living apart from family convinced me I needed some type of exercise. Not just become the couch potato. We can pick up the pace a bit, Cathy."

"Walking is good for you. Walking is very suitable for drawing air into the lungs. Except we do need to watch out for pitfalls."

"Pitfalls, like what? I hardly notice any. You sure about that, Cat?"

"Sure, I'm sure. I came within ten feet once of a pitbull, motley double teeth all showing as if grinning. Of course, I crossed the street in a hurry. Cars have also suddenly come too close. I've slipped so many times on cracks and rocks, I lose count. People should keep their dogs off the street, and a driver should look both ways before turning corners. These cracks need fixing. I suppose the benefits outweigh the consequences even so, Saddie."

"Me too. When I was young few the consequences with less people owning cars or dogs. The three of my teenage friends and I would summer vacation weekends walk downtown to Union Station. We'd sometimes chat the brief discourse with soldier boys waiting for their train to come. There was little fear of what could threaten us those days. Once I walked alone to the park across the street from the station. I met a young soldier walking through the grass there too, since leaving the Soldiers' Memorial Building off a short distance. Suddenly he stopped to turn to me, as we were walking, to make this confession. "Of all the soldiers in my barracks, I'm the only one who prays. "I thought, How Strange. What about you, Cathy?"

"Strange indeed. I never heard that before. You should have asked why. Except, he may not known the answer to why."

"So true. Up ahead where we turn, Cat. Next I see you I may drop a few days off walking outside. I sent for the DVD tape to train me how to walk inside to music playing."

At One Convention

This will be one grandeur night to remember, John. These women came dressed right for the occasion in their gauzy thin jumper pants, floating chiffon voile gowns, bangles, glitter necklace here in Vegas. Did you see the woman who wearing blue flash evening dress trimmed in marabou fur. It looks like waves shoring up on sea water, especially when she walks. Of course, the men look swell too in their dark and lighter toned suits. These tables even dressed swell all in pristine white tablecloths. That's the one-man show signing autographs in the aisle. He jokes, he sings, dances, plays 3 instruments. Not too good on the xylophone, though. After the 4 man quartet sings, it's on the program African man American poet we came to see up next. The scoop is anywhere that he reads serious poetry, he gets a standing ovation outdoing tall those funny comedic poets. Look at this brief outlined menu, John. It offers no braised vegetables, pepper jack ham, salad, not much of anything this night with Poet Convention Week. Just frosted cake and coffee.

The Concussion

Was he some kind of wacko nut quack doctor? Who was this black man to tell them what kind disease had the retired NFL player got? So said the NFL Brain Injury Committee in year 2006, 1 year after Dr. Bennet's findings went ink jot published in one Pittsburgh journal. Who was he? He was and is the southwestern son Nigerian doctor who studied in 3 universities, one college and coroner's office. He holds eight stamped degrees and board certificates. His mind then was sharp as the dart hits target right dart on the mark. But a football player could he get a concussion? Yes he could as Dr. Bennet Omalu so aptly found out of one player man who was retired, depressed and destitute to the shame of nowhere to live. But his mood sometimes wondered of helmet heads game grabbed so. Suddenly, the player dies in middle age, the killer Tau protein brought on by the game's blunt force to the head tagged as culprit. So said Dr. Omalu after studied his brain was main tissue. Soon another player's tissue, the another player's brain broke down. He and more players boasted suicide and death, which in 2009 led to unrefuted proof doctor claim was right. Football concussions are real.

Chronic Traumatic Encephalopathy CTE for short, tags the sore brain disease, "It kills." No more doubt.

THIS FOUL WATER

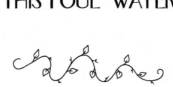

Ellen did you hear about the water scare many folk this town about all out scared our house taps could run putrid brown water stays tea colored rancid like in Compton, CA? "Yes, I heard news of that brown yucky stuff running through sink faucet people of Compton scared about. I thought it localized there. Where did you hear otherwise?"

It's true the harm is localized there. But I hear it on factory job and MTA Transit how people in town everywhere getting anxious the same thing could happen any parts here.

I stopped by to see what you heard.

"All I heard is what was in the news. That city had the worst so long it's time for do what county officials lately doing, even to point of switching city board due for other county members they afford."

I agree they should. Officials put somewhat blame on manganese coated pipes befoul water works stained. Water should be pristine pure always the same. I've even tasted in my own faucet water the bleach into ·w a. t- e r so strong I can hardly stand the bitter edge in taste. If I even leave it in the frig a few days the bitter taste yet lingers. Leads one to wonder of what else contaminates house water and why rivers that polluted?

California has one catastrophy after another that other people don't know about or see. They think California a safe haven, Land of milk and honey flowing like an oil pipeline. If only they knew about the fires, mudslides, high rent, overcrowding, let alone earthquakes we witness here. When drought comes, we have less water to live on. Some areas run out altogether. And we need clean water everyday.

But enough about water not all it should be. Let's talk about shopping downtown where the latest green cell and i phone in stock.

"I'm for there if you are. But why should those be green in stock?"

Just a fetish of mine. I hear so much about green-house gases and global warming I try keep something green around me. Those potted herbs, I'm sure you've seen them along with my prize aloe still rising up in tall aloe vera points. Keeps my house air fresh. Don't forget car keys. Ready Ellen?

THIS GIFT HOW GAINED OR LOST

The band leader of orchestration
The speech is of who orator
And hold to promise have in trait
The intent given with strike palm.
Elation smiling assurance it stakes
As if these vows won't if break.

And promise all they keep.
And when they break, Eden willfully weeps
To some their even losses reap.
The author of secrets men robbed,
Common laborer lost his job;
The Band leader won't keep.

I once vowed to write everyday
Poem I'm down to simple this way.

Bemoans of Sick Days

Sherice: (Beside the kitchen) Guess what? Today sort l been telling you a sort for hard pull.
This morn, I had release in was this hard
I could swear by a dentist the ache needed more anesthetic till cavity of extraction
gone with a tooth pulled.·
And nose run wrenches sneeze in sinus drip triggers main it upsets tremulous the
stomach unsettled. You can tell it bungles feel well day when beside here I am
dinnertime cooking meal while somewhat my predicament acute in these pounds,
pounds in overweight. Besides, brain gets foggy. These ill ways are the pits.

Ardella: Appears to me bulk weight of this wise it crumbled
Did not you lose a few, lately, in pounds. I could have sworn. Besides, have that,
too, loss of memory. What do you weigh?

Sherice: Ridiculous unsettling pounds in least they just remark of stout was flush with
stopped weighing months ago.

Ardella: Something could stir habit to realizing proper again. Custom I, too, have days amount feels go tremor of nose whimper makes me feel bad myself, sad case of pollinated dust, smog, smoke air pollution drab say of each cause. I have who aunt has endocarditis. Nil know much about it 'cept for suffer in the heart makes her weak half time she feels which inflammation burns. Add to that her ankles swell. Predicament we' face, this truth, it grossed sad. Our hope the wage better, perchance it changes on tomorrow.

I Should Have Been Happy

I should have been happy there. And I was, in town half country where for living in the little frame house. Beside the kitchen window I looked out I saw how much rabbits loved eat carrots right source right for the fuzzy wee tan and white coats. I should have been happy there. I loved the smell of fresh cut grass, cut grass blades low for little lad and lass children mine spring and summer play they to romp with red wagon and cavorted with toy fun. Big mulberry tree burgeon picture superb then where some had plum and peach tree to the brim. I should have been happy there. But vision grossed love city mirth more where escape is from the half country how most gray on mirth to flourish past mate died. Though city living, too, would peak and pale. And live alone would steep in gray length.

TIDY UP

The Taiwan bowl crack and rift, chipped mar,
No fond of prim attempt heaves from gin bar.
Staunch china vase imported, nil, the rust,
She'll half care if relic grand in dust.
Side table knickknacks have some nicks gored.
Like ceramic seen inside hard boxes stored.
Exotic duds tail their European prints
Cramp the metal frame of scar chair rents.
Ever creeps out where of every turn I took,
I spied the bruise adorning untidy home look.
She's not rich nor long for cheapest brand.
Grim made blame she testy won't stand.
Train this woman how smart to be clean?
Coach the Far East grave war is mean.

THE DATE

Ethel, my mother, was helping me into my dress. "Hold still," she said. "No need for wiggle it on that much, even if it is the trifle inch or two snug." She was right. It was a sky blue chiffon dress that fit a little snug around the hips but floated above the knees in a flare down 5 inches below the knee. She had helped me pick it out from the corner garment shop in the Market Street shopping area not far from where we lived. "It really is a pretty dress· I must admit, even if I did have a hand in the choosing. You may know what's better, but in this case, mother knows what is best," she bragged pointing a finger my way. "And you thought it was too long!" She would have to brag as always when she approved of something this beautiful. "Alright, alright, rub it in, but I still do say the dress too long. Goodness, it honestly is not all that cold outside. Shorten it, Ethel, please. Neither one of my thumbs appropriately suitable for needle and thimble." "Neither are mine," she said, shoving her head to the side and looking straight dead center in my eyes. Besides, next hour your date is due." Ethel was separated from dad and lived residing a while with her mother in St. Louis, Mo. where we both had hopes of meeting the right guy for me. Mr. Nice Guy turned out to be Rudolph, nicknamed Rudy. Rudy was medium built with slightly broad shoulders. He was a delightful to look at, be with and talk with yellow skin young man who boldly stated our first night alone that he was the one for me. It pleased me liberally that his love for me was that strong and that immediate. I was 16 and he was twenty in those 1954 year days. Now into 3 months dating, this was to be our first night for going to the classic frills and necktie theatre for which we had to look spiffy in something special, meaning no casual skirt for me and no Levi's or rumpled khakis for him. This time we were putting on the 'dog' meaning finer suit pants for him and luxurious chiffon dress for me. And sky blue was just right for my complexion was neither far dark as ebony dark nor light but somewhere in between the two. "Now all we need is the chauffeur to drive us," I said to Ethel. I was all dressed and ready to go when came the knock on the door. It was Rudy, of course, all dressed up looking dapper in his light brown suit pants topped with three quarter length loosely hanging overcoat revealed a dark brown suit coat was open enough to show his white shirt and, Oh yes, the beige mixed color necktie. "No need to come in," I said. I hastened on my white wool coat and said 'bye' to Ethel as I immediately stepped outside facing winter in the air. "Decided which restaurant we'll be going to?" I asked Rudy as we walked to the bus line nearby. He hunched Up his slight broad shoulders before saying, "Umm, we can look around for one after we leave the theatre."

Around 8p.m. we finally reached the theatre was out a distance on the west side of town. The classy theatre ornated with lion statues flashing red eyes on two lower step banisters was more than I expected as we sat down on cushion seats of velvet like tapestry to watch the movie. I don't recall what the movie was about but only recall it spawned no complaints just only a tender ecstasy behind the one and a half hours.

As next we looked for the nearest restaurant, we found one open that was Asian. We had stepped no farther than 3 feet inside the door when the waiter immediately rushing toward us got near enough to say, No negroes allowed. We stood a moment, our tender ecstasy shattered even after turned on our heels and left. It was my first encounter with prejudice.

Day With a Certain Hunter

How many times had he seen the rampage. Tony, the federal inspector chief, greatly so had seen the menacing rampage as much as 15 years the length he worked the job long dear to him cannot it disarm his right niche. Where savage breed to hide in crevice many, he keeps probe sight on rude swarm the rampage inscribes vast the infestation sum. Even if they hide in bored in holes of wood in thick forest and folks yard goods. He's known for even climb a yard fence, vault over bramble bush or boosting self atop abandoned furniture for top to peer into binoculars just to spy bulk crop of a coast hides the bark wood robber. Tree bark ramblings each year destroy mass trees. This day he hunts the Long Horned Asian beetles rate won't all stick to invade his home town streets rife with trees of New York. They this elusive to hide on cargo ships to Chicago, Los Angeles, and else cities.

Some people ask, "How do you work as a chief rank inspector here so many years? Don't you dread of work around such infection?" To which chief pluck said "It is demanding job take gut. Someone has to. If not me someone another. As for be infected, this I'm fitted with protection company gear." Tony has a sharp eye for signs of infestation seen for oozing sap of pitted bark goes with here today inspector worker of a will survives beside these block by blocks lead his will down dim basement steps, up fire escapes, do check under barbed wire all to scrap specks like roach specks few town folk know to care much of here Brooklyn. No will to stop eradicating beetles marks him like detective scurries venom encampment rampage from keep since how disarmed by craft his chore he rank for like breed rank for beetles make so. Suddenly, the middle aged woman frantically shouts "Help! My basement filling up with streak white fly wing roaches the looks of which unsightly bunch that I have never seen before."

"Those are no roaches, Miss. What they are they more the Long Horn Asian beetle. I must flushed them out enough to fly into your cellar window no doubt was open." True to word it was open. "Thank you she said after the beetles eradicated wing bunch gone. "All in a day's work," he replied quick to scurry to the hunt this beetle hunt day.

It Patterns Male

Depiction has a man
For black and white the chess piece where
Each player plays the L shape square.

And scrap the void is none, no stunt
He eager than the pawn he mystifies behind knobs.
Move the chess piece across the board, he won't sobs
With add his bliss to will and won't.

The face expresses of a man
He opes for no disguise to friend he checkmates,
Kind is not perfect every trait.

And generous with he gifts her a frill thing
His game approach to mate rejuvenates back
No hard posing, unlike the board this packed
With black and white pawns, one up around king.

Depicted like a man you can know,
And gamely by a certain king piece site
He may sway game approach to he cares how the move to the right.

Don't Lie to Me

Alice said it plain to Marge, I love me. Me, myself and I of such to lie won't do. Now, here a quest I sadly ponder through, why so my doc prescribes not enough I see the meds to weigh on keep what health I pride. My beef more or some stronger meds I need. On earth, today, knows many a dead heap. One doctor likes to say some folk don't eat. Marge, would you love just gulp down juice desired. People say to drink water a lot to which another doc ascribes to do not. Because it deletes potassium count. I can do with love some harmless jests glee. But man or doc much duty on keep us healthy, I counsel you, don't lie to me.

Minstrel To An Orphan

Young little orphan sing a song
Lilt of how the opera fares
Since, lo, you left the common home.
Lilt of lad if love it cares.

Set your minstrel aft the strain
Graceful patent bard at pose.
And set your minstrel wrote in tune
Graceful tune could yet, be chose.

If, near, I come before you when
I hear the song you worded tone
And if I like the song you sing,
I'll sing you gained a better home.

AFTERMATH OF A HERO

Arthur had been home, now, since June, 2007 and was amazed how the land had suffered and still was. In places, it looked so downright crusty earth that he wondered when the rain would gush enough. Still, he was happy to be home where his hopes and purpose for living were as firm as his renown.

Everywhere in town people recognized him. This was easy in a small town like Statenville, city where everyone knew each other's business. So, anywhere he went, people would praise and applaud his army courage along with the knowledge that he won a purple heart. Even in the little clothing shop he and his younger brother stopped in and browsed through items were some on racks and stack on tables, there too it was no surprise when store owner, Mrs. Gilligan, couldn't help but remark, "Such a brave young fellow you be." "I was only doing my duty same as any soldier would have," he replied. "But it wot not just any soldier who subdued 100 men 30 of whom were brought to prison camp," she returned. "True, but I had plenty backup supporting me. I was just the one who ran out in front of my comrades," he said. Arthur's 12 year old brother, Dave, who had gotten fed up with hearing his brother all the time being lauded said, "Yea, anybody could shoot like that. Hada been me there, I would've shot down more'n 70, myself." Arthur and Mrs. Gilligan laughed. Almost immediately he flashed back on how he lost his leg was badly shattered between that heroic combat.

After browsing around a while, they started to leave the shop when Mrs. Gilligan called to Arthur before coming over to pin his tee shirt with the red button said 'Our Hero.' Arthur thanked her and with Dave limped through the door on his pros- thesis.

Weeks later a cooler Arthur reflecting was glad for the cool spell that eased up a scorching dry spell in the pouring down drenching it took the night before. As Dave abruptly burst in home, he could-hardly wait spilling all to his brave big brother, since both parents at work. "Guess what" he said, "Walking home from school, I saw a kind old lady slip and fall into a mud puddle of water left over from last night. Soon as I seen her down, I rushed to her side; and after helping her up, she remarked she had never seen anyone so eager in haste run just for help an old lady. With that, she thanked me and gave me this good luck coin." Dave held up the shimmering coin. Arthur said it sure was gleaming a coppery blaze, seeming to blind his eyes. "Good for you. Now there are 2 heroes in the family!" said Arthur.

That evening when mamma mending Dave's socks and poppa doing nothing special, Arthur decided to spring on them his plan to look for a job. After it so stated, mamma the first one to remark that she thought it was too soon for her first born son to start working. She had rather he'd buy some nice clothes, have fun on the town, and relax for a spell. It was then poppa in southern accent of his exclaimed, "Lat a boy do like he wonts to. He aint no dat gum baby anymore, and he ken drive my car; I sho as corn husks won't mine." Arthur began to ruminate momentarily on one saying must be true, that you can't unaccustom the south from a man whichever location he moved. But he knew poppa was right. Ever since he could remember, mamma had often doted on him or underestimated things he did and seldom blundered a chance to make decisions for him. Now, here he was a grown man who had served in the army for two years and last, receiving an honorable discharge. He loved his mamma right enough, but at age 23 after serving in that atrocious world of savage combat, he felt he had earned the right of make his own decisions.

Arthur had been at home, by now, for 4· months and had had all he could stand of sitting around the house or going for the weekly walk or engaging at home in yard work. By now, he had his whole heart and mentality in look for a job.

The first place he drove poppa's car for an interview was a paper factory where, immediately, as he walked inside the wood paneled average office room, the quick gazing supervisor noticed he had a limp. "Don't worry about the limp; I can work just as hard as any man. Soon as I become more facilitated with my prosthesis, I won't even have the limp" said Arthur. The super looking dumbfounded said that he was afraid that Arthur didn't understand. Hell, what was there to understand? thought Arthur. The super went on to carefully explain that with this job he'd be standing on his feet a lot and have lanes of paperwork to stack. He couldn't imagine that for Arthur. "Do you have a resume?" Arthur started to answer him like he envisioned poppa would say "No, I ain't got one. If I had one I'd dam well show it." Instead he said, no, sir, while in his heart he shouted "I'm a man, same as you are." He could barely hear the super say, next, he could only hire people with a resume. So, a bewildering Arthur left and headed next for a truck station.

On his way there, he passed the once admirable lake and felt sorrowful it now carved in dehydrating mud. Quiet memories flooded back of him fishing there many times with poppa. The lake was healthy looking, then, and brimming with tiny aqua greenish waves. Would science at all remedy the water shortage? He wondered when and how.

The super who ran the truck station was even harder to convince that he could handle the job.

He wasn't positive how long Arthur would last with driving nearly everyday. He felt his prosthesis leg could only obstruct likelihood of having the job done precisely in time allotted.

Arthur could not fathom where to turn next. He only knew he wasn't ready for calling it quits, not until he received some sort of confirmation, verbal or written. So upon almost passing men constructing a 3 story building, he felt he could do some simple task like help unload the wood, mix concrete, tote water, just something. He stopped the car, got out, and asked for the supervisor. After someone called for the boss, Arthur was having second thoughts because of other supervisors shallow of heart. He had gone to as many as five work facilities and was, by now, verging on losing his cool. Doesn't anybody know empathy for the handicapped these days? he thought. Although he really didn't want pity. But any emotion was better than what disturbed him about unaffected supers no right emotion while looking dumbfounded. Afterall, other handicapped people had gotten jobs. Since only his first day out, he must not lose patience.

The 5 minutes went like 15 to Arthur. The super came arm in a sling reminding Arthur of a handicap. He gave his name as John Benton to which Arthur replied, Arthur Clayburn. He asked for a job, explaining he didn't mean climbing lofty ladders or endangering himself on framework's ledger. The super thought a minute before saying "Oh yea, believe I do have something. You can help with painting the rooms. They're already done with building on one story. Leave your telephone number. I'll keep you in mind for who to call soon." Arthur said thanks and left his number. His heart pounding in his throat, he went away thinking, yes, yes! Finally, someone cares, and had humility enough to hire a person with a handicap!

Allow Me This Claim

Leave me alone,
Let me do what I want.
This is an awesome day to be in,
Stuck in a room with sense, my friend.

Countenance calls--
How low the orange flames
That cool the first in fair earth leaves.
And pen and watch be not amiss
As I will even get enough of this.

HARLEY BOONE

When Harley Boone came home to live,
His life was in his room.
And few the times he'd peep and peer,
And scarce the noise he'd commune.

Then, rose the mood he'd raise brick roof
For tramp cane up and gone;
And none assayed what Harley laid,
But, soon, the arighted tone.

And past the mood by anxious room,
Forbearance needs foretell
How like this day will Harley Boon,
Will cheat the sad awareness knell.

THE THOUGHT IS NOT ENOUGH

Because in mind won't always sell,
That in itself be not enough
For soothe the harm I'm, here, to tell
That hurts when go gets rough.

A time you woo the hand to hold
Be near the blooms in lovely hue,
Will touch a time when brainwork told,
"To love is more than ideas do."

Then, hence, the thought is not enough
To sell my bill of goods the right
To call my mind in consort bluffs
Than draw the love it craved in sight.

LOVE

As blue as under skies
When rude malice the vein.
As rose for beauty flower
When jollity for gain.
As gay as some are widows
When they concede
To value affection more.

SIXTEEN TO 75

Did I date? Child yes. I'm not too old to remember that. I decline to say much of the first young teenager kind but could have been kinder, a trait he had time to learn later in life. My second one a teenager 19, got a little agitated when I who sixteen asked him to wear something less than casual. Wouldn't you know he showed up wearing Levi's and leather jacket did not match the new dress and cream color wool coat I wore. I had learned in high school a date's outfit should match up with what one is wearing. His defying my request made me a bit irate then too. Still we shared the fun evening in the movies nobody could see how it was we were dressed. The next and last date came for whom I later married. We went on dining and movie dates and to whatever wrestling match we liked. He was kind, considerate, a young man of good manners. Sometimes on our way walking from a date, we stopped at a park where I posed as he pretended to take my picture with make believe camera. If snow on the ground or we more breathing cold air on the bench, so be it. It never bothered us one iota. We were in love, we knew. I was 16 and 17. Those years, I never thought on growing old except to wish I'd grow old gracefully. Now that I have grown older, I wonder if I crystalized that wish. With growing older the years go by fast. One year comes in on the heels of another it seems to my ageing years too quickly. And friends I had I sorrow over most now gone. One died of a stroke.

Another one died while listening to music. She liked music, any except symphony.

Another died peacefully, heart just stopped. I remember how she repeated words like hello again and again and other words again to people. Those her last years, her memory half shot to smithereens.

The one who died of lupus came with a menacing rash, isolated herself in her home for years. Just did not want people prying or infusing their well-meaning advice into her condition. She had a doctor.

I isolated myself in the 3rd floor attic once too after my husband passed. He was 36 and I was 28. I left a decorum passable home to go live with my mother again. I certainly had to be depressed. No words else define my attitude. I just did not wish to commence upon the light of day. Finally, I realized I had to. I thought next of go college bound seek a career but by now I was developing vertigo. Still ventured out somewhere. To the movies, to restaurants all alone. I shopped the department stores a lot for new clothes and eventually took a trip. It all kept me alive and active between then and now. My capacity at age 75, I'm a client at Senior Center. There I meet people the same as me. Some are widows, some widowers, some ill, some handicapped who still they join there and participate whether happy or ill. This life is enjoyment, suffering, and death.

Would you say so Patty?

"I'm only seventeen I've not yet lived long to know."

Me From E to H

e   I am equal with the meadows, the fields, the bay,
the sidewalks in grass turf.
I am enlarged by even many genres
discover turf has worth.

a   I am airy as the day borne breaths you breathe.
My shyness light and gentle
may turn like crass and swift seen the hawk
Then much I am belligerent.
Though too I do give life.

r   I am rampant raging as pitapat drumbeats
or claim brilliance in the shower.
I pound the drops if even pound not liked
in every rinse the hours
I march for man and beast.

t   I am tree green as oak, pine, sycamore of tree
I joy to spread my stands
so like the mantle dangles richer shawl
of me will sure to dance
and aid in cleanse the ozone.

h   I am humbled of the warmth favors less cold
in the rejoining way of spring.
I am known at dainty flowers pile hillside
God and man cherish me.
I am of heat I am of nature
I am of God I am of worldwide

A Storywirter fantasizes—How Another Began

Storywriter —I say that chap on myth had story lines myth he wrote at even, corner cedar edge. He was like me the other one, myth writer, 'cept barb wrote down instead of burgeon ideas churned and ticked abundance into ink, he slowed on scribble theme. And started on at table height his slowed on theme. Decided, he for 'Mystery of the Grecian Urn.' It stood on counter pane for British taproom he phrased a script in bar best belongs Pub. Since Pub by other name simply guesswork, of becomes Nearby Tap, a tag for late, some bushed out tippler selects his own tag. Now England here the writer was born. But early resolve he of abandoned trace of odd urn, but set his saga vase first out of Greece before it reaching Rome where might a mood writer become his epic barb renown chap essential in town once for Empire. He knew the rimming urn, dead man's keep gore chrome it once selective for some dignified ash cup the one they mourned by buried dead had cup it stood for ash Greek Official and Greek priests ere it, next stood it seen for sleeping dead the keepsake jar at any frame for counter top. For death hath nothing obscure from rank what comes to, each, one and all.

But last that chap began his thoughts like mine. Except deep mystery of own adapted plot meant for sure, that chap to, next, cut phrasing short, and rhymed long story plot with short on length he cleared some stops as due clever barb.

Alter Ego—Now, since I was 'fore this about I write the bing, long yarn, among mildly mystique on how the wide brim revelry cup thief was caught at folk's own brick and backstreet shed, I think I'll veer the switch.

I think I'll make next one a Keats.

THE POET'S FANCY

Sometimes, he'd ask himself, say what of roes?
Might he walk, trek the haven where,
Where lilacs wave and cocodette goes
At ideas hope and wolds despair?

And if who travels 'low the vast blue sky
Go vouch, for a trait under sun arched tall,
A mead is green so meekly painted nigh
Treading will tread for trait recall.

His painted around shall echo swift deer
Who run, bypass, in seam brightest vales.
Of castle corona cavorting near,
Steering will light on gallant skirt dales.

If gloats to modest smiles most vivid
And kiss to Eros genial pleat rose,
As mouth be reddish, cry ails be livid,
Hearing will hear out coral lips those.

And if he pants when tell and rate
The victory assayed by warrior victim,
Who sailing to attack while stake the mean slate
Gets verse on grave the grim war to win.

And what can do more for what we show?
Our writ by word if vast and small
Shall pen the mark if high and low
For bard will air all for thought recall.

Of a Willow Tree of Late

Oh slender willow tree falls
your branches are bending bowed.
Your limbs from grace are
breaking
as heeled to how slips
allowed.
Since our youth departs
from pride
had yields to all first
avowed.

The leaves are dry
beneath you
rending with less early
glow.
And reared up slighted those around you
are left with gray the bushes
glow.
Fair looks accorded once
my own
of fades where strapping hairs
rate low.

Your willow hunched to autumn
torn
though birds affect dreams on how
offshoots drive.

Desires aspiring folk want off ageing
test age
may strain for past youth
alive.
But strain they losing push for
they
resolve in, God, let age
thrive.

THE BLOSSOM TOUCH

When bluish blues touch blue bell hips
And orchid light tempts jasmine white,
He fondles skirt at yellow curve waist
Where is that flower grace ceremonious
No formal ritual voids embrace.
When saffron trees twine deep jetty roots,
They bridle tied will feast dark dense denied
Our blighted mental truths.
Where white blue grayish and bright tapestry,
Her coral red shawl into limbs they united.
With petals clear and no grave thought applied,
Do they deface the worry with men excited.

SUMMER FUN

She likes the ivory tusk behemoth stunt
Where show for crowd to watch,

Hurrahs the go with marathon run
Where folliage greens hedge route;

Would hie for torrid bushfire espy
Though he espied scene with game park.

And joy would cheer for warm florid land
As glee alone must hail parade the march.

She harbors tree by gleams daffodils,
He's all for hedge surround shade the yard.

But neither hey about how August ends
When zone for summer jest is done.

CASTLE ROCK

Climbing in the hills a sort for wet sponge
Had granite prime in rock chief boulders
Chief One and two inset the porticoes tall
In long tall of annexing joint on joint.
The long house crafts had the works climb
Where near wet the sponge banks for wet footprint.
Now, stately rooms were rooms steep with a stalls
Under splendormost gallery sort in broad
The wide extent. And now who with guests of castle
How odd it raised is the owner regaled beside talk
Of manor style or if parodys 'Noah's Ark';
That aft where they inside some have it airs
In love with sleek silverware and high graces
For air this next "My, how it thus and so grand."
And banquet room this flash belongs with decked
Chic tux on chaps' dude suits, and lady vogue
With sipping sips of wine 'neath much for how gleaming
The cut glass flicks a chandelier burns
This flash ornamental for owner has much.
And those who lacked, nil, from discern it more
Were into in and out around castle
Much for all spy or all assert a cause heard
After his turning them to his attention
Behind cement stairsteps he gave them lead.
Since, he known for not only stout of things
First to face but stout of yields into foresight.
And stalls took shape below where those behind
Were not a mite behind steps a tall stairwell.
For straight up and up in cellar's backroom.
Stalls for the shelter stacked each the high tins,
And jugs were every type paraphernalia shelf each,
Each ranging keg stacked for the rumble in mind.

No farce in that if that indeed put for his hunch
Now, that one owner lived awhile but soon demised.
Then came a day the rumbling digs ricket grown aged,
It grossed it 'cedes to shakes and rock resemble
Rock castle to the ground rock, stock and barrel.
And quaint of raze castle none raze he had in mind.
Food for thought, here, if one prepares for war
It could some other jerks take preeminence.

No More Kids

Have you noticed it much dear how my income is? Sometimes I make a lot, sometimes earn less than enough. And this we do have 3 kids. The way my paycheck is I venture right out say it here, we don't need anymore. A couple we know in our church has this rate of one every year. Why, is not clear. One day I said to the husband, What? Are you trying for a dozen? I got no response to what.

I deem some parents discover this, how little kids don't require much. They don't eat a lot more, even don't care to even know what fancy clothes design about.

Of course, change course they will in later a few more years. They will equate with their peers who crave and get goods galore. Then is when our expense becomes more.

ABOUT WHO SITS IN

Something about who sits in
The wit between the wall and closet
That makes it look you could pin
Just by the way the shoe for set
How a far particle came to rest.

Serenely ceiling standing den
Mindless of how a naughty ambush.
Rushing, did it fall from poke star bin
This trail affects authentic rush
Of parcel forced where close at cliff bough bush?

Nodding to the wall, I know
You have no say to say at all
Than these are feet in tongue upon toe
Too hushed for how the rock from shafts tall
Devoutly, had to split and fall.

This is a lonely place to be in,
In without a fall record book;
Or the right of one companion then
Who'd help me mark the meteorite look
Or save me from the fault solitude took.

LADY AND THE TRAVELER

The traveler came at night evinced snow,
He had no cane but dun black crow
And a case that was sealed
And for his burden filled.
He knocked where swiftly came her nimbus
Expressed to him some gift and thus
He wished her gift in a silk ribbon chest
There for the years request.

Exhausted tired from weary his trip,
Ere he asked he whirred by the hip
And saw night could go long
With whitest stars flaked on;
With traveler and his bird in flakes bare.
Except he sought whose charm stood there
Where two were him and her,
"What if two hearts the magic were

I stop here awhile my bird and I?"
Her tongue said "Traveler, I won't lie.
I have no husband spouse
Nor help who tidys house.
Designs this cold and drifts' porch top,
Who tells if swifting snows won't drop?"
Then winter was blown stern beats somehow
Stern rapped and pelts a window row.

Lo, she abashed remarked, "Oh, I'll
Allow you rest if, Oh, for awhile."
Chill night, she let him in,
Equipped him brew and some hen
And whit a crumb for his dark crow caged.

His yen was quietude but play engaged
These tads by burning stove to and fro.
One stood to say hello.

A woman free but 'cept for lad and lass,
She pondered case and by a lit pane glass
Construed if case amounts fold
Conceal if weapon black gold.
She in her fear said, "traveler, out" who went
A poet and his crow in swift snows sent.
And he could not he tell for all her brood
If e'er she wed or if she lewd.

My Going Radius

Going, I can go. I've made up my mind.
I'll take my leave from street the road
keeps the lane way of where my bind
Kept me stamped in all diligent chair.
Now, I'll expand from there,
Say short adieu to wall placard
In debt to so great as my seminar pays
With script notepad deed my task guard.
I'll tip the knob way of how my tip
Says "Here's to split. That's that,"
So off I am for where beach land.
I'll take my chance with trait wave sprays
Wet bouncing vault with hunt wet sand
Made void and null the weaving dare
That sunk me in the spin marked chair.

Lerner Brown In Vegas

When Lerner Brown tripped in Vegas,
So near he in this way
Between swig men of started fuss
Were high on beer had sway.

Among those sat where table slot
For hotel grand casino,
A brawl broke out amidst two hot
O'er chips and thus and so.

Lerner got slapped caught in the middle
One fist to crack, dazed chin.
Befuddled of head his luck got undid
Rocked by one of two men.

Then, Lerner fled his hard earned merit
Had learned he'd dodge and duck
When men assail their adverse hurt
They do their cryptic luck.

This night, occasion gained his trip
From fluke life had height.
From where he left his poker chip,
He learned let bad men fight.

Some Died

First one husband mate I loved he died.
A second one and 3rd were main boyfriends died.
The few off kept the wooing strong, they live
With try to get it right, some blame in diet.
On earth it summons us to diet do.
I once on stern that diet strict so
I stayed had to at quieter home bedside.
To live, to die, to diet. All get sad dull.
We know which one will sadden us worse.
Live long as hope for on earth.
Such we should if we dare.
Someone loves us for much our worth.

CREDIBLE DISCOURSE

Mom: (Quick entrance at livingroom) Oh, there you are. How of specifics gone, today?

Angie: Specifically, they averaged around to rank with the average in this way for the subjects more. the content would brief curriculum, this and that. I think passed if most assuredly the English. Such entrance exams beget gruelling task.

Mom: Beknown, you had it semblance hard choosing, but had a choice decided, yet?

Angie: I fathom, best, in my degree of chojce yes and no. Yes, for in seeming how it scuttles courting lab degree it halfway hurries yes and slows of crushing say no to master of art. Decision making, it adrift between the two.

Mom: Choice, it comes to that. If you pass exams and if you aim go where college distance not far from Rock Peak Mountain people hike, make sure you take water along, occasion you there if lands on tour.

Angie: That much amount I do if, even, on boatride.

Mom: I know that, dear, but water is good for something. I read, of late, it carries every herb, vitamin, food, pharmaceutics, even, to human cells need repair, recourse they must in order they thrive survive. Besides, it even, also, flushes out the kidneys. A concentrated type I never even heard of before combines sodium with calcium chloride and, too, magnesium something of wet sort the call pronounced as Crystal Catalyst I may of order sometime.

Angie: Gee, mom, thanks for the info I never hear the same. This for one of two around listless half tired, perchance you headed kitchen way, bring me a drink of water.

His Time to Move

Soon, will they build the passage herein
where, here, for some with riving bar
the land for who should rive the soil they mar.
Paps, you gotta move, move away from here.

All rose flowers hang where kept.
In vision keen this lovely image seems felt
an image poised where staunch profile once.
Was it not ruth day long the vintage left
the wrath of soil to wage of, here, sadness fell.
Her bed is doubtless, yet, colored thread spreaded
where standing by the foot, here, frame posts apart
where standing nigh events she's appalled how
decking the threshold of dowager mirth
attesting to the wound of cupid's fall dart.
In picture pose have here, his stance
with gray delight she had bliss day he seen.
And wrinkles, too, in gaze of care
discerning how her way of careful to glean
yet a sly ease upon her picture pose.

Gal, peep, now, and see if pale violets yet
be rising in the garden set erect.
And that tall palm approached to violets left side,
has that substantial lifted root, yet?
And those lit hillocks dingy cliff silhouette,
as be they everywhere in town,
will eve that pertinence go down?

MOTIVE WITH HORSE RACE

Of, here, a gait Patricia will yell for galore.
And calm the pack where none the steeds deplore
examined first for spirited hoofbeats, nil, shaming
horse on hoof a glass magnified for how hoof in frame.
"Patricia, peep look see if all inked of number ending."
That much meant for steed ticket in quest by a friend.
"Concern I have too if the digits clear for each one seen.
And this aside, my number odds in fourteen,
times I came if to yell the shouts had thrill in yell.
Truth now I am bereft of housework wet swing
I could swing mop a turn to do if pick to choose.
But face it work is work. Be here how steed fuses
this heartbeat of mine with it pants quick pant
benear group steed this keen on any day enliven race."

"I thought you random go that intrude."
"Go which? Oh, here. Of course, I do else choose
the Bible I won't rule out tho days for skip verse
sort of direct me how escape. But, here for odds amount
sweet curse
it idles guilt since race horse odds in win each time
rank with almost. And only ranks me fool if 'mounts
I losing everything.
And count of who 39, four of which years if vice
in few bets, I grossed I just lost once, well, say twice.
'Come on, Seaweed Bay!' Last month, I lost many
amounts of dollars a hundred on Moonlight Rider.
I should have known better of bet on slow strider;
tho much on yell it speed if, even, dud lost race or two.
If, in case, I do win, of wonderings unsettle it what do."
"I were you, a warm day for buy the voile dress
shimmers dandy."

"You would say that. This notion rambles in best hat,
it, even, favors purse and for pick gloves to match
for, in case, busybody nosies what I bought.
These winnings nil enough for car or own trip I ought.
'Cept I could with length save the reaped sum.
"Pat, look, your horse won.
Not bad for woman places bet, now and then."
How to make discourse short, it 'mounts to who glad of win
here measure, this time, it had lucky winner main.
I have the feeling another odds will have main
in racetrack odds of she could lose again.

THE LAST GOODBYE

"There, you are now.
You sneak you in there now.

"Hush, honey babe. He in there sleep.
0kay to look, just let him sleep."

"That scound of whom sleeps."

They had embarked upon near enough
They could see he was her father
By name on the stone.

Her husband looks beside not to cower,
"What is it you dread?"

"'Scoundrel in there, now. It had to happen"
Came next.

He could tell something of how the pains
With almost ranging frowns on her teeth
Or by the mock hardening led him remark
"Don't. Don't look so if it hurts."

He moved how closer 'side
The arm about her shoulder slipped around
Much out of touch who needed this comfort.
About what, slip none, yet, said.
Most he suspected most about fear.

Who much unwavered went on
"It none groove enough.
No grave is groove enough.

I don't see that it all deep dug
Amounts for keep scoundrel."

"Dear, now, honey babe stop. Just look.
Just listen at yourself.
Something just different.
You told me otherwise before."

"He had me thinking me, me I the one
Blame all these years."

"You told me other about father
Parent of yours the other this kind:
His kindly gentleness of took you places,
Bought you things swept from just you imagined,
And if you sick he held your hand.
Nice kind man.
Remember? You did. Or less you remember."

"Yes, I did, said it then--before last week
I held up swept from gentle in the paper
Demeaning text, same, like mine human text."

"What subject, sweets?"

"Shish. Hush you up I'll say."

The scald rays breathing dragon on wavelengths,
They sought for bark of draining heat with shade
And took the shaded seat from stone how engraved.

She rested head where on shoulder slipped
His times head up had slipping times down
For she then said on "I remember well
It all too well. A cunning sort that
If I should call him that, even, behind night
Remembered that, now, I recall.
I do remember staying which l stayed
In rustic off limits house of housed me
Twixt I was there case the weekend
Uncommonest I spent among some other visits

Stayed of since parents lived they separate.
That night. Oh Grief, that night
l fear to speak!"
Now, she somewhat sobs on her teeth,
"I had stuck feet in from crept
Between the window from his corn field,
Corn growing outside I had this urge.
After this back--in truth defrauds sleep,
Blame of who came, some sneak about he came
Entered where I, back, laid across my bed
He sneak for entered in into my room."
She sobs now, in her tears, "Oh Blame I can't
Can't go on. These things unseemly!"

"Then, don't hun take to heart so.
I can guess the rest what happened."

"You always phrase that same you can guess
At even other talks we down to meaning.
But I must…"

"No, dear, don't if it hurts!"

"I must. Must say it anyway,
I must. He raped me.
My own kinsman did things. Unseemly touch.
Beguilings had of 'What' and all at once 'No'!
Can't stand it all. Squawks he would have heard before
Along some trifle I mischevious,
Now, no, to deaf ears. And next the rising
Beneath the covers just kept rising.

"Strange differing from his loving parent
I thought I knew him. Meaningless glory,
No sense him twixt me my weak twelve years.
Dear mom she ne'er however sharp
Suspected anything, even, aft l brought home.
Too, sneak he never said."

Her husband had his maze guesswork torn,
He sliding arms from slipping him closer asked,
"How many done to your ungraces and why?"

"It happened only twice.
Luck or child one approved me worthy.
He must have seen the child of how shies
On, even, they were other visits past.
My blaming self for him or sometimes me
Is how mocks me behind
It every since I thought me ore,
Blame me more every guilty age twenty odds.
In answer to this, why, endows searching.
Otherwise deeming I should say
And you must knowing deed comes of innocence.
Your father tells you child do a thing, you obey
Not knowing he would changing down deed
To self indecent."

"How better rid of it. Let me in to you,
Help block the worst. Let me help have you better, somehow,
Without keep worst this so much blame."

She drawn compelled to mimic worthy
To husband what once she held from she answered.
"I should let you in to help shame. I'm willing,
If what demeans me ever my temper so disturbed.
His truth he never sleeps, somehow.
But stain behind the stone, Goodbye.
Now, I've said it.
It's in the open, now."

WORDS TO THE FACT

The squalid house
the tacky blouse
the stripped lea
the wretch in dim cast bird;
all deemed the svelte this bare
as summons deed around autumn sleeps.
And deems what rooms around poverty
it assessed of,
Poverty is a fact it wants order.

Assessed Of Wealth

The plush way couch, the decked out garbs,
The lavish chaise lounge, the manor odds.
And wealth is all for seen that when
The sound passerine resounding plush spring,
The budded wet dew seen on blooming rich bough seen.
By day, the member rooms 'round sweeter themes tweet,
By night the rich room with tie gray nights to weary sleep.
If I were rich deals, true, I would for own wealth.
But who sweet on rich deals could own comes next.
This member next now the one who losing sleep.

Along This Tenet She About

Some little something 'bout him she could see
Some little sum in had his motive right,
Since, chief, he likely had his wont the same.
Each several days uneven thrice a week.
She, somehow, knew for likely one reads where
If she had slack time she sat for sips of mug coffee
Such the mite rooms and sly brushed along winter
Blown trite at eaves for someone living under.
She slides on coat becomes almost on.
"When mother was alive, about she small glad."
She said to Carloe still in the kitchen.
"I think she lived for this, anon, I arrived main
If much for own brief speech in mother tones.
And these were scaling where they cushioned slight climb
She moved from the rug, waste to her, books to me.
And laughing chins left others for she scolds
'Untidy heap' to her. But how relate of known
They had to stack what small addressing jumbo stack
Mom took for blame prodigal addressing row stack.
That was dear mom for mother graces odd
If then she never stopped there with tidy bookwork.
And how first one thing led to another
That time she said, 'Belle how'd it go today?'
I had just only, then, begun—when was it?
Oh—then was months ago, nine for exact
With teaching you to read
Before true as she gone she passed last month.
And when she here wont made it out
Belle was not my own as wont to know."
He walked him in who entered from the kitchen
of Spanish ilk bred grounds from Mexico
Gave grounds to lively shirt mixed colors rouge

He saunters of and heading found
His lounge the one where young man under a roof
He sat for none forever ere he stood.
For since she standing said it outright enough
For surety of it mimes heard well, "My nickname Belle
Is not my name. Alike her mother stead
She would none dare hear me unbless her mom stead.
Granny, ole wretch decries foster mom, I never said.
She still none too old age then at seventy odds.
I keep this label on odd just that."
He had his own whose living had something to look see
If hush chief in live hush on her bed.
"Is she still…"
"Yes, she still, yet, peeps 'neath the patchwork.
Every once in a while she wonders
Just leaning there
With leaning on her side
As if she longs go feel the breeze
Each rummage through they plaster coast across
The grounds that suits how blooming fine in the west.
Just sad, this much longing who paralyzed
With eight too sad each month mom lay there
Borne on her back too much bedrest between.
Longing, it shows she longs, too, youthful days were best.
"No I don't feel I'm fit to see she flounders.
Frail mopes impose upon me glooming."
She said this for he had asked her look in.
"Prone am I to hello. Hello. Peace then."
Sounds went unheard. Quietness.
"Or prone to she'd say she was well."
She had it coat for starts leaving out
When he said, next, "I'm too glad that someone
Did leastwise of something you were here for.
Where else but in this country can it be
the English dark face something of her here
I have it kind? You were here for me
Latino speaking language how you say.
Now, that is like the dream, in truth, bargains."
Carloe spoke his English how said breaks down
Bit he much learned from her teaching helped.
And had his struggle 'long each every whit

Latino put his heart in own of well read
Puts drive in one belief, right, had ambition.
"It runs with least the bargening struggles.
Who puts teeth in believe in teach, at times
Lets me in to humane. But where, where else
'Cept in this country where born
How I am 'twixt my English spoke from dark face
And one, another blanched skin how he is
That even since and after language annexed barriers
For crossing over, where else
That after who wanted learn, I do humane well since
I teach? And next humane it happens kind
We both each none regard for color.
It happens where but in this country."
With that she walked on.

More Sayings

Age and youth what shall we say of two? One is more blessed than the other.

The rich for have more, the poor for have enough. Money, Love, Happiness all count.
Beauty comes, beauty goes.

To think, to read, to write all reward. Age lives for living.
True Love never fails.

Words worth remembering are usually sweet. Work ethics the key to opening a shut door. Spring and fall rate for seldom too hot or cold. Children have fun if sunshine or snow.
Harsh words hard to swiftly fly away. A kind compliment stays long.
Writing poetry is like fitting pieces of the puzzle. Religion--men confess it, study it, but few live it. Know yourself.
Love brings Peace.

We all want Love, Peace and Joy.

If eat and drink all I want, it lacks for something. Give me a comfort shoe to fit.
Not all dreams come true.

Talk while walk with someone, only talk slow. The right clothes fit just right.
It feels good to have a companion.

Eating right underrates eat fat meat a lot.

Summer comes for have fun. Be frugal since debts come. There is a time for spend more.
Drink what you may, but don't leave out water. Work but don't work yourself to death.
Don't cheat sleep.

Propose to me with the real is no fake diamond. People who listen hold much to talk about.
A painting tells you something like does a note. I have a painting I almost figure out.
Air too polluted is not fresh. Go in, go out people say.
Stay calm, get angry.

Smile but cry only as needed. I walk but still gain weight.
One day I sing, another I groan.

I can't always abandon complaint. The sun won't always smile.
Too much clutter exists for reduction.

Music has what rejoices the soul. If life seems a challenge it is. Don't under -estimate poetry.

THE RANGE THAT STARES

The range that veers the stare
Can petty be the hemlock coheir
Abides with surface pose you pair

With one of gallant look
Compares to posing so like the mare
The fore rock little forsook.

And since it angles stare
It veers dim syndrome, no doubt.
And casts the gloat wily there

That forward gaze to roll omen
Weird from grooved front like lens
The panes for hardly wear good grins

About puts me bit in suspense.
With candid symptom sash pulled back.
Concerns me how the windows wear offense

'Til last this want to vanish.
And how severe would wee fret get.
Still, stare it brings on panic.

This haunt that veers the stare
Amount could sole assume small damage
If just with stare the only dare.

LEFT OF ONE PARENT

A noon is here
and much it seems to peer
the one who lives her home out of reach
She matched the bough sticks, one and each

with tucked her brood away from sun
inside the little curve with mother one.
'Til beaks to whimper their cries went unheard
when off she fled like flee they heard.
And left this house to whimpers fate
like children having but for one they wait.

LITTLE GIRL WITH A PASSION

She in her move for young passion
Thus, had scale if one by one
She let go forward in walking
The soles crossed hill she was on.

Erelong, she paused where open door
Plateau evading rich and fine
Since, next, she saw this wealth belied
From rich at the stairway climb.

"I must be lost from, one, the threshold
I cannot find on my way
Or else I have the numbers wrong
Removed, here, gloss from rich lay."

The woman stood on heard her crys
Asked her digs her small girl far.
When told said, "Ah, you have it wrong.
Number you seek in far door."

At last, she went her sulking way
Crying and weeping along
'Til, next, she met a door opened
Defaced her sad, sullen song.

Now, lo, behold bejewelry charms
And, Ah, for silk happy turns
Tho they lapped and decked by dusky sills
Becomes what rich madness earns.

"The wealth is as I heard about
But down from crave that way north."
There's nothing wrong with ends you're for
If, last, you end by go forth,

Rimer On The Road

Rimer on the route to who knows where,
Sometimes this seeming how I care.
I met a lad where a far modes lie
He stood him on the road nearby.

His skin for sandy paltry hand
And tans ascribe him paltry stands.
Except he gazed and I for one
Mistook him none the homely son.

"Piper, you can make tones ring
Pipe the rare as none, no string,"
As I may quote, he added phrase
"No violin contemns the praise."

I have no flute, how can I pipe?
I have no pipe, how can I pipe?
The pouch is case where homage lay.
I have no pipe, how can I pipe?

"Rimer, wealding pipes are read
Sole with just they ring," he said.
"Else the right airs in strings to flex
Are violins tune the song text.

Be thou equipped for deeming here
Coppice for slain as hangs this clear
Sing me a song as confers wish.
Rimer, Rimer sing me a wish."

Just these fades as near me knell
So drear these hang than conferred swell.
And if so fall this trite in sight,
I wish whatever falls removed from sight.
I'll not lose track of then my walk
I'll go where some augmenting stalk
Marvel round if Oh fragile garden hem
With how the walk in lack for dim.

No Boulevard I miss at last.
And travel Ole route is vast
I hope the one less fault I stay
The blooms Will chase sad dooms away.

I stopped for speak none else it came
And started on route the same;
But when I looked where lad would be,
His lad peculiar vanished he.

Eschew Temptation

As traveling on my route, one noon,
My test was of the dread or whom
The wicked saint for so earn me fault.
But quick from lust, discernment I thought

Fret in this day I live alone,
My knees are best shut than open, prone.
I dare not free my love just yet.
I dare not; except for the love true the asset.

DISCERNING LOVE

Hush, all ye heavens stop your crying.
Here, is the love in kind undying.

I will not lose my child, away.
I will not bruise my child, today.
I will not cause my child who weeps
I will not cause a deep sleep·

The Struggle Goes On

The struggle started a long time ago and still is going on. It is a struggle for the benefit of the people since we do have certain rights.

These rights were first initiated under the written affirmation of the Declaration of Independence. I'm sure Abraham Lincoln, our 16th president, was all the more stirred into action by the justifiable words that all men are created equal and are endowed with unalienable rights as life, liberty and the pursuit of happiness. Aren't we all entitled to these liberties. I'm sure Lincoln could not see how people could keep on living with part free folk and part indented slave, slave folk branded by fiery hot branding irons like they used then to brand cattle. A country divided against itself cannot stand. It's not easy to imagine that this even going on back then before my time. It was not right.

Others felt the same way. People like Frederick Douglass, a slave who with play pals' help taught himself to read, left his slave master and became a great articulate orator who spoke against slavery as repulsive and needed abolishment. That did happen during Lincoln's reign, but slaves were not altogether free. Some big wheel masters still shackled them with slave labor on the farm and plantation.

And before they became free, women were in the struggle too to help free them. An emboldened Hariet Tubman risked life and limb to transfer willing slaves from the south to the north where there were more freedoms. What a brave vanguard for civil justice. When people would hear of her courageous gallantry stealing slaves from the south by way of The Underground Railroad, a foot path, they would say of her, "Black Moses is on the war path again." And she was a Black

Moses. She helped over 300 slaves to escape to whatever freedom they would experience in the north and was said to have never lost a traveler.

Then also was Sojourner Truth, a slave in every sense of the word having no education. She was so in the movement for abolishment of wrongs that she changed her name to match the journey she would travel from city to state to administer speeches. This time the war path traveled on was not just about slavery but also about womens' rights. Her speech she proudly blasted men about "Aint I A Woman," at the 1851 Womens' Convention that also included men is realistically brazen and to the point. Her moving and undiminishing statement concerned she is a woman who could do things for herself stays with you. Women are not as weak, so deflated of energy as there are men who like to think so. Many have read her speech and have recited it, including myself.

In those naughty 17 and 1800s, many men designated wo men as home bodies too fragile back and dermatone for any thing but housewife and birthing babies. And birthing babies they did. Some had between 6 and over 12 children.

It is acutely noteworthy that other women got in the battle for rights like more and equal pay for women, the right to own land, receive custody of their children in divorce settlements and womens' suffrage, the right to vote. Of these brave women were Susan B. Anthony, Elizabeth Cady Stanton and Louisa Mae Alcott. For their brave gallantry, women are without question thankful, since we benignly reap the benefits.

Still there are conquests to win, borders to cross; as witnessed by the civil rights bill radified because of the efforts of Martin Luther King Jr. Still these demands for increase hourly wages, better race relations, residence for the homeless, more rights for women, rights for minorities etc., these each owns a link in a dour battlefield. Hence, the struggle that started a long time ago is still going on.

LOST IN DISPORT

Why did little Benton roam
Up and down where tripped and fell
Over ground started on the peat moss comes?
Blue mischiefs, bleak, never tell.
Up and down where climb rebuilt
The fickle disport stairstep town.
Up and down, what the heck, guilt;
I lost it, my silly frown.

WHAT KIND OF LOVE

This one portends of Love. But what kind of Love
when Love takes you to movies,
dinners, and favorite trips but lips
do seldom pucker a kiss.

What kind of Love
when your mate gifts you somewhat nice
the jewelry plus dollars a few
and helping hands touch but arms
of a fashion few the hugs.

It's kind if bed work briefly curbed.
But what kind of Love
few the kisses,
few the hugs,
and how bed performance equals nothing.
What kind of Love,
What kind of Love,
What kind of Love.

YOUNG LASS AND I

Young lass I met on the lonely track,
She had no purse, no loose hung sack
And drifted with the whimpering wind
On winds of a close edge to send.

She walked behind me, first, silent trace
Then, quick off saunter, next, hied pace
Would clear me on how precisely go
Since, now, swift case the walk from slow.

Now, two for crossed o'er this traffic light rank,
I aimed of which, sage, just fit for thank
Her tot had gazes curative smile
on dim my thanks by the tree in style.

About for to board by the lane had bus,
I saw the haze finches eve had, thus.
Which salve was kind was disappeared gone
In all her kind like child my own.

My little lass where can you be?
Fallen is not slipped on the pebbles fee
Nor falls on cracks pitted into lane
The builders left nicks in springtime pane.

Trusting not far I fear a grave eve
For you may roamed so far from seen;
Not knowing where you emptied cry
Such night a wee chirp sounds hedge nearby.

Then, on to felon stands the scare
Drew sword and crys to shudders lair,
Your tears be crying weeping
Afraid a sword would bring deep sleeping.

But, then, I looked, saw mitigated seat
The lass of on filled and, here, to greet
Behind me 'side the night was in firm,
The child from gone had come safe return.

SOUNDING OUT SPRING

Harbinger of the dyeroots bleeding red chants.
A tendons of the dandelions cheery stance.
A feather of the downy brook sneezing in the cling.
A thrust of yellow tanager of favors fly the cast sling.
And every air is crested on it hoops grass theme.
For these are timely opus of we stand here between
Class piece for soon enough it rightly scores intrude
The temperamental chase convening on, prelude.
Engineering of minds rate how tunes in warm air.
So many set for to ride snappy chorus clap the fair
In axle hoops carve groups of trail ruby graceful owns
Of dewdrop bluest jays game loud to fly on.
Anxious in eyes will have less to late crooning
Accepts the dark hours night along soothing.
Now, sounding it owns to gentle glow to note
A nightjar pipes quieter stealing milk a goat
A piebald neighs to land on pelted hide
A cow of low keens with nipple tip guide.
A child of these goodnights of doze sweet,
But no one for the mom tucks her in is incomplete.

As The Wind He Traveled

As the wind he'd take the gadder's roam,
As the wind did shuffle he.
And, sure, the whole he sought to seek
Must, yet, discovered be.

He'd ride the wind the rolling blue
For what could suit him swell,
And ride to where he'd shuffle more
Where came to where dwell.

As tripped in haste for open fare
Where leisure made her camp.
Why, he'd feel free where breezes fare
Prolonged from a building's cramp.

In outdoor yields in raceme air
Served to revive his soul,
Tinted with moss who'd lie full might
Upon tint bed behold

And met with seen of rays how Kneel
On valley maid attire leas
On day sheet how no ardent breeze howls
Her stir on shady leaf trees.

Dusk trek or light he'd bare the ears
And sounding went the 'lease
The wild indignant beaks had trill
Tipped feather trill release.

Beside a doxy to addle,
It set in courtesy galley
Despite how trill in trolling spring
Had toot toot in song yatter.

The more he came to visit which
A far out camping zone,
The more his want to yearn here visit
His grand and pretty Yvonne.

Unlike how scene of his a far field
recessed no indulgent lark,
Where here the paltry picayune cold,
Weak chill halted wail remark.

Oh, bonny plane, Oh, seamaid coast,
To thee he'd take right toast
To primrose red or green sea fair,
The one or both award boast.

Be, here, the coast he'd live the toast,
A trip from work of brief wont.
And, here, survive 'til travel ends
Behind maiden last for own front.

As purpose suit her bank it rank
For island suit her fling.
At orange heat skirts the hulas bonny
From near and far come to swing.

Oh, island scene, Oh, bonny scene
That having its own right appeal
That hoop skirt dwells at primrose scene.
For, sure, it's grand you'd feel

To spend a turn to pleasant yields
There on some far off coast
Where green sea wave where coast for greet
Anxiety, none, wretched boast

Where bucks and gals are more than pals,
And fellows, who do, have their pick.
Some galoots choose one. some mate two,
For habit consuetudes pick.

The simple mat and eves that beam
But contact post and room
That had it much shone neatly buffed
Could first delayed some gloom.

The dainty maids a dish would serve
A dish and rich of taste.
Since boardroom served tight barracks,
Ripe melon feed unwasted.

A many tripping member resides
With somehow this board homestead
With dust on stained the gloss wardlike
And light blue tinted beds.

And many nights a yokel thought
For campsite scene outdoors
Where hopping pleat fins will scatter
And branch the bough pleat soars

Where spring his constant companion
Where yet few troubles ail,
And dreamed the scene where primrose blue
And verdent sea chilled on dale.

But molten sun for finding, none,
No mere warmth for own last slate
Be, here, his trap would buck and yearn
And buck and yearn and wait.

It seemed to Remus sparks would stay
And dull his wait forever,
But hailed one near of summer molten,
A certain for heat to weather

(Hold onto all the view you've seen
And listen to the next)
And telling how whose legal release
His measure for more rest

Left him by, one, kindred uncle
Of sums beloved he grossed.
Behind the plushest city tower where
Doth staunchly, now, he'd boast.

Like wind his pleasure to and fro
And, sure, he'll tell of main
The wind it ambled where it would,
And where he may dare roam again.

Arabia After Dark

John--I' m gratified I came.
The spring has made it right.

Abdul—Such springs renown here.
And other springs a caliph's fountain cascades.
The springs and court he lives add thus long age his
If even though, anon, the rank
In right stead, after him begets a caliph one
Replaced by who next one could age his life

John—Have seen in spring else how things else do
As, too, your caliphs do. Such grandeur with nature ranks
Like mainly swells the life in things grow like tall
Those knotted panicles yon window height.

Abdul—Meanest how the white yucca?

John—I had about the name, but a view
This tangle bush in white panicle flowers flush
If even from a several tables for seen how right
With since we dine. And since it mimes class
It semblances of a psalm it fills the room.

Abdul—It has no bearing 'side from white.

John—(Lifting a spoon) Must still it rate
And so invite us here, the same,
The same as high walls in sight.

Abdul—Did you know pal Jamel the Fortune Teller?

John—Since we just, only then, just met yesterday,
I could not know for here-to-fore none said.

Abdul—By now you know and henceforth thou know.
He is a Fortune utterance by it clads
It ranks him wise 3 seasons Prophet so clad.

Jamel—True, And who thus and so wants rate
Should for derive moons many more.

John—Then say the words in what put
For proof the sage knows of my whereabouts
Some here and yon and yon to there since true
The stranger in passing terrain Semitic.

Wrinkle Lady—Whatever do expression well, so do, so all may hear.

Jamel—By right, I should. Would sounding lip tone
Land on ears stay agape?

Wrinkle Lady—Alas, 'twas no concerning lip tone
Nor firm, and naught for would have said
Except the feeble noise would sometimes raise.
But add for all ears hear.

Jamel—I'm glad you held for this adds on
Directly motive I'm about. (To John)
This much from having heard in passing time
You, John, here, from tripped afar from
It brims motive of where upon an edge built.
Now this no one had said, current blazes beam
Of edge walled or if moved heap solar beams down
You've come afar, again none said, from off
A broad turfs average shakes and weepy mists
Alarm public of the hills golden place.

John—You mean California.

Jamel—'Tis one and same. And other those prevail
Have in orange orchards abrupt shoots grow
Almost like ocelot haste of Texas, and grapes gyrate there

Around seeds sweet meat haste.
Be you keep melded help about a store thither side
For local winery, choice you left son
In league with overseer. True to, here, stranger who
Said it yourself. But pass is at Arabia goes
Through to Israel. Go, even if anon you lack for go.
A stranger you are as odd manner I've seen.
Since your lack when merger of matters urgency
You lacked take steps restrain a store from doom.

John—(Resting his drink) It can't be so what heard.
A man this met again, here, dusk tips dark
Who placed where I'm from and somewhat else do,
He semblance in mite wizardry sage of words.

Abdul—Was every said just so?

John—Every wit.

Abdul—It rights an early quest, foretales this true.

Jamel—Alas, I'm not thus this right or wrong always,
But never the full prophesy tees off.

John—(To Wrinkle Lady) How moniker you attired how
Attached a nickname?

Wrinkle Lady—It was no pick in self choosing
Nor given at nativity, but at length label caught on
Like hinging or to charm fair looks
Like how some fruit wimple marks do for tell thus and so
Of how ripe the fruit love sweet in each streak.

John—Blemish love?

Wrinkle Lady—yes, love, some have they best define
The manner assessed this wimple mark
With this they to say best of Wrinkle Lady how
She aging mature with gain long years in how share kindness
What makes good of wimple mark.

Abdul—(Lifted a spoon) Look Jamel holds a rose.

Jamel—Only one rose now two, now four.
Did anyone tell five?

John—It has your Genie I can tell.
For I'd just now your rose compare same to yucca
Each limbs in horny so. They both in tough limbs
Alike to crafts I've seen except for flowers off same.

Jamel—As Allah Islam's man
A Fortune Prophet some bit of magic learned
His age lavender ago

Abdul—Aye, that purple as tunes do night-owls do
Of sounds would overhum the wolves.

John—And this you know?

Wrinkle Lady—It already if said.
Intense iris purple.
His noons were doom, yea, eves that sad.
He never wanted magic but lack in wealth
Endorsed amounts sane past came to sentence in him
How gloom keeps mainly doom.

Jamel—This fuss with magic, then, doom,
It served me with undeserted zeal
Deserted logic fires the soul intent
I fixed daring with friends I allied with
Though mainly of good intent.

Wrinkle Lady—But we did notice came this rut
It anchored in mainly moody by noon or night.
Jamel—But in ramrod circuit those
Certain ideal should lending aid of toss rut
The grisly scorn from aid who ill diseased.
Is it, hence, namely, allies unison for?
But figure a rose it crafts flower.

Abdul—It decks bloom like cunning maidens more appealing
When time is right.

Jamel—(Of sips a brew) Cunning, well see for self
It tilts, it waves, it bows.
It less this mite concerns work or either play.
In circuit earth these simple sown much they bloom
Of hue ornament them right. What best suits
Than loveliness and peace that since our lineage
We crave more. (He leaves the table, talks with someone
Before turns back.)

Abdul—For sure, how thick gets burgeon sort.
And sort prized here at Wrinkle Lady's crop of dents
Approach to once we've seen the lark
A tannin rose outlines of sort
We never cease to wonder.

Jamel—(Returning to table) Ahoy, everyone off,
Desist off bud types
Lest news unto John nil directs my say.
The city from which you've hailed with sad much in
Epidemic the one is split, the lake disheveled heave
Of such you ofttimes feared the rent.
Where shook the first side of thine for moiety place,
Some few are dead as, too, by nature's law some wounded.
And serving law on this wise, turgid winery 2nd side
Now, crass the weird grapes of gyrates crass
Quake must vents of crowding moments more into.
But the disorder sort inclining on could be the worst,

John—(Excited) Tell me no more a sorely grave fortune,
If Allah stands for God and Messiah if hears me
I less for doubt nor fain would now I believe.
In temperament Hamlet style, to do or not to do my quest.
To wait a while or travel some quick way back, this hence
One thing I do or void; and added say in fortune you
The prophet further said had outcome awkward since
The harm came unto occurred may too pained my son.
Although a son I plead is naught for injured or dead.
This fare of eat and drink it weighs somehow
Amidst dark same as no sight realized in how blank.